CRAFT

POEMS

Printed and published in Great Britain by D.C. Thomson & Co. Ltd., 185 Fleet Street, London EC4A 2HS.
© D.C Thomson & Co. Ltd., 2003

ISBN 0 85116 831 0

£5.70

3

The Cinderella Mum

by Isobel Stewart

I was all set for a fairy-tale night out with a real-life Prince Charming. The question was, would we find our happy ending?

"STEVE will be coming, of course," Linda said casually. "Steve?" I asked, even more casually, as if I had no idea who Steve was.

But not only did I know very well who Steve was, I knew exactly what Linda was up to. Finding A Man For Megan — it's her latest game. She's a crusader, my sister, and right now this is her pet crusade.

It's six years since Tom died, and she thinks I've been on my own long enough. Well — as much on my own as I can be, with three children, a dog, a cat, two budgies and a hamster. Oh yes, and a goldfish.

"Yes, Steve," Linda repeated, firmly. "He says he wouldn't think of missing our silver wedding, after being our best man. I did tell you he's divorced, didn't I?"

"Oh, yes," I reassured her wryly. "You told me — quite a few times."

Linda hugged me. "You never know," she said.

Three little words. But as the silver wedding came closer, I couldn't help repeating those three little words to myself, like a charm. You never know.

We'd been happy, Tom and I, in the short years of our marriage. I missed him, and part of my heart would always belong to him — but six years is a long time, and in my most honest moments, I had to admit that it would be nice to be married again.

5

It would be wonderful to have someone to love, someone to laugh with, someone to share the good times and the bad with again.

And it would be particularly wonderful if that someone was Steve . . .

Twenty-five years ago, when Linda and Frank got married, Steve was their best man, and I was Linda's bridesmaid. I was just 18, and from the moment I met Steve, I knew he was the man I had been waiting for and dreaming of.

He was 23, and seemed so mature, kind, good-looking and funny that I thought that all my dreams had come true.

And then, at the wedding, he met Linda's friend Helen.

Helen was the same age as he was. She was slim and dark and sophisticated, and when I saw them together, I knew I had lost Steve.

Throughout the rest of the wedding, I hung on grimly to my pride. I held my head high, and I laughed and I sparkled — I think. And it was only when Steve came to say goodbye to me, that the sparkle faded and the smile slipped.

"You were a lovely bridesmaid, Megan," Steve said gently. "And some day you'll be a lovely bride."

I shook my head, all at once unable to speak, and I think that then, for the first time, he understood. For a moment, he was at a loss. Then he took both my hands in his, and he kissed me, gently.

"You're very sweet, Megan," he said. "And very young."

A few months later, Steve and Helen were married and they moved to London. I didn't ever see him again, although I heard news of him from Linda.

And, of course, quite soon I was able to smile at myself, and my foolish dreams. I met Tom, and slowly, sweetly, our friendship became love, and by the time we got married, I had pretty much forgotten Steve.

But now, with the crusading gleam in my sister's eyes, and the plans for the silver wedding party going ahead, somehow I found he was very much in my thoughts.

"You're very sweet," he had said. "And very young."

Well, I thought, as I looked at myself in the mirror, I'm 43 now, no way could he think I'm young now! I was on my own, Steve had been divorced for three or four years, we were both mature people, and you never know, we might just find there was something when we met.

The possibility spurred me on to take myself in hand. I borrowed Jenny's skipping-rope, and every day I skipped until I was breathless.

I stopped using the lift in the office, and ran up and down the stairs. I bought a rinse for my hair and a sleek new dress for my sleek new figure. I was ready.

"What do you think?" I asked the children a week before the silver wedding, as I paraded regally into the living-room.

Three pairs of eyes were glued to the television.

I switched it off, and stood right in front of the blank screen.

Three pairs of eyes were now fixed on me. Well, four if you count the dog, but I didn't think his opinion counted for much.

"You don't usually wear black, Mum," Rob said, a little doubtfully.

"Will it stay up?" Peter, the practical one, asked.

"Smooth," Jenny said with satisfaction.

"Thank you, Jenny," I replied. "No, Rob, I don't, but black is very . . . elegant. And the lady in the shop said it suited me, specially when I let my hair hang loose. Yes, Peter, it will stay up, it's built to."

"Can you walk in those shoes?" Peter asked.

"Of course I can," I assured him, not entirely truthfully. "I bet it cost a lot," Rob muttered, and I knew he was thinking of the sleeping-bag he'd been promised for his birthday.

I put his mind at rest. "It didn't come from your sleeping-bag money."

He had the grace to look a little ashamed.

"Well," Jenny said firmly, "I think you look beautiful, Mummy, and I think everyone at Aunt Linda's party will think so, too. So there!"

Not everyone, just one person, I thought, as I hugged Jenny and switched the TV on again. Just one person. Just Steve.

You never know, I reminded myself.

And I said it again when I arrived at Linda and Frank's the night of the party.

You never know . . .

STEVE was already there when I arrived. He was standing at the window with Frank, looking out at the garden. They both turned round when I went in.

"Hi, Megan," Frank said. "Linda says would you check the things in the oven, she'll be ready in a minute."

Unobservant, my brother-in-law, and I was glad of that, because I didn't want Steve thinking there was anything special or different about the way I looked tonight.

Steve came towards me. "Megan?" he said, unbelieving.

"I told you she was coming," Frank reminded him, but I don't think Steve even heard. His eyes took me in from the top of my flowing hair to the tips of my very high shoes.

Suddenly all the skipping, all the racing up and down the stairs and all the money spent on the dress seemed worth it.

Steve was transfixed.

"Little Megan," he said, wonderingly, then hastily corrected himself. "Well, not so little, really." My eyes were almost on a level with his.

It's the shoes, I wanted to explain, I'm not really this tall. But I knew that the elegant and sophisticated woman before him would never say anything like that, so I kept quiet.

"You've changed," Steve said.

7

I laughed. I'd practised that laugh — light and lilting, I hoped.

"It's been twenty-five years, Steve," I reminded him. "I've grown up."

He hadn't changed much in all these years. Oh, his hair was beginning to go a little grey, and his face was thinner, but the years had been kind to him.

"Oh, yes," he said now. "You've certainly grown up."

The evening wore on, more guests arrived and I stood chatting to Linda.

Steve was at the far end of the room, talking to other old friends, but I knew he was looking at me.

Believe me, it was very flattering.

It was a lovely party, and there was such a warm, happy feeling about everyone. Yes, it was a lovely warm evening, but not much chance for Steve and me to see each other alone for a little while.

No chance at all, I was beginning to think, when Linda reminded everyone that the big basement room had been cleared for dancing.

Steve came over for me right away. I knew he would, somehow.

"Dance, Megan?" he said and all at once I was that 18-year-old Megan again, breathless, cheeks warm, her heart in her eyes.

I reminded myself severely that that was a long time ago, and then I thanked Steve, lightly, and went down to the basement with him.

THE music was soft and low. There weren't many people dancing yet, and Steve's arms were around me. It was good, too. Very good.

"I heard about your husband, Megan, and I'm sorry," Steve said. "And I suppose you heard Helen and I got divorced?"

"Yes," I said. "I'm sorry about that, Steve."

I wanted to ask him about his children, if he saw them much, how they had taken it, but at the same time, I wanted to keep this time for us, for Steve and me, without memories, without questions.

But Steve wanted answers.

"Linda told me that you have three children. That must keep you busy," he said.

"Oh, we're very well organised," I told him, airily and untruthfully, shutting out a mental picture of chaotic mornings at home.

"And you have a job too, I believe?" Steve said then.

"Yes, I'm personal assistant to Mr Graham the lawyer," I said grandly. Well, it suited my new image much better than telling him I was a half-day typist.

We talked about how the town had changed in the years he'd been away, and how it was living in London. His arms were strong and confident around me, and in a convenient mirror on the wall, I caught a glimpse of the way he was looking at me.

All very satisfactory. And yet — and yet —

And yet, I admitted to myself, with reluctance, we were like two strangers. There was a distance between us. Maybe it was the 25 years, maybe it was more. But it was definitely there.

And I had to admit something else, too. My smart shoes were becoming more and more uncomfortable.

I longed to kick them off and dance without them, but, of course, I couldn't. I was far too smart and chic to do a thing like that.

I don't know whether it was the shoes, or whether it was knowing there was this distance between us, but I just knew it wasn't working. There was a lump in my throat and I felt so empty and miserable that to the next few things Steve asked me, I could only manage a nod or a word in reply.

I really don't know what I would have done if Jenny, my youngest, hadn't phoned.

"The boys said I mustn't phone, Mummy, but Matilda's had her kittens, and oh, Mummy, there's one little one that looks so ill."

"I'll come home, love," I said. "I'll be there in ten minutes."

Quickly I explained to Linda why I had to go home. Then I hurried out, glad I'd parked my car at the side of the drive.

There was, I have to admit, one moment of regret, as I drove away from the lights and the music, but only one. It had been a dream, that was all, there had been no substance to it, and it hadn't worked out.

Jenny was waiting for me, a smile breaking through on her small tear-stained face.

"I should have waited, Mummy," she said, as she took my hand and led me through to the warming-cupboard where Matilda always had her kittens.

"I should have remembered that there was one like that last time, and Matilda just had to lick it warm, and then it was fine."

We kneeled down together to examine the tiny, newly-born kittens, careful not to touch them. There were four of them, and they all looked fine.

"I'm sorry to bring you away from the party, Mummy," she said. I gave her a reassuring hug. "That's all right, sweetie," I said. "I don't mind."

Half an hour later, all the children were in bed, and I was happily and comfortably in my old pink dressing-gown, with my feet blissfully relieved in my battered, comfortable old slippers.

The one thing I wanted was a cup of tea, and while it was infusing, I tied back my hair and washed my face. Then, my mug of tea in my hand, and the dog at my feet, I made my way towards my favourite armchair.

The doorbell rang. I groaned inwardly, trudged to the door, opened it and let out a squeak of surprise.

It was Steve.

He looked at me, and I looked back at him.

His mouth twitched. "Cinderella, I presume?" he said gravely, and he held out my beautiful black shoes.

"You left these in Linda's drive. I came out to say goodbye when Linda told me why you'd gone, but I was too late. The coach had gone, and there was nothing but the glass slippers."

He looked down at me. "You're much smaller without them," he aid.

Slowly, the full horror dawned on me. My old pink dressing-gown, my shiny face, my hair tied back.

"You wouldn't have another cup of tea, would you?" he asked.

SILENTLY, I led the way back to the kitchen, and poured tea for him. He sat down at the kitchen table, easily, comfortably, and after a moment, I sat down too. The dog sat down at my feet, and Steve bent down and scratched his ears, absently.

I liked that. I like people who are nice to dogs.

Steve put his mug of tea down and smiled at me. It was a slow, warm smile, and it did the most peculiar things to me.

"Now you're more like the Megan I've been waiting to see," he said. "Oh, you looked wonderful, but you weren't the girl I remembered. You were so cool, so distant.

"Then, when I heard you'd gone rushing home because your little girl was worried about a kitten, I knew you were still that Megan. I hurried out after you, but there was nothing but the shoes."

I had to take it in bit by bit, slowly, carefully.

"You said you'd been waiting to see me?" I said, not quite steadily.

"I kept telling myself it was ridiculous," he said, a little awkwardly.

"But from the time Linda wrote asking me to come to the silver wedding, I just kept thinking — here I am, and here's Megan, after all these years, and we're both on our own, and, well, you never know."

I looked at him, and a slow, golden bubble of happiness began to rise somewhere inside me.

"No," I agreed, solemnly. "You never know, do you?

"How long are you here for, Steve?" I asked him.

"Long enough." He reached across the table and covered my hand with his.

"Linda tells me there's a family celebration tomorrow," he said. "She's invited me to come to that, too. I'd like to meet your children, Megan."

Suddenly the old pink dressing-gown and the slippers and my shiny face didn't matter.

"I'd like that too," I said.

Steve stood up. "I'd better go," he said, reluctantly. "It's late."

"I suppose you'd better," I agreed, and I didn't care that I knew I sounded reluctant, too.

We walked to the front door.

"See you tomorrow, Megan," Steve said softly.

He looked down at me. He didn't kiss me, but he touched my cheek, very gently.

I stood at the door watching him walk to his car. See you tomorrow, he had said.

I said the words aloud, and when I caught sight of myself in the hall mirror, I noticed I was smiling. ∎

He was
looking for
romance —
yet it was
right
there,
before his
very eyes.

There Are None So Blind!

by Shirley Worrall

MARK was building a pyramid of magnetic silver stars on his desk when he heard the crash in the outer office. He sprang out of his chair, all set to investigate, then thought better of it when he heard his secretary, Emma's, voice raised in revolt. "I don't know why I bother coming in here . . . no-one appreciates me . . ."

What on earth was up with Emma? Should he say something?

Puzzled and shocked, Mark returned to the safety of his executive chair to consider the problem.

For the next half hour, he listened nervously to filing drawers being slammed shut and the shredding machine being kicked into life.

Mark couldn't understand it. In the three years Emma had been his secretary, she had never once appeared harassed or flustered. She was always calm and super-efficient, and now here she was slamming filing cabinets and shouting irrationally.

Suddenly he heard the alarming chink of china rattling on a metal tray.

There was the briefest of taps on his door and before he could draw breath, the door opened and Emma walked in, bearing a tray with his morning coffee. "Thanks, Emma. Er — everything all right?" he enquired tentatively.

She smiled sweetly — too sweetly — but her eyes said, if you're too stupid to know, I can't be bothered to tell you. "Wonderful, Mark. Just wonderful!"

She spun on her heel and Mark watched her walk stiffly out of his office, flinching when she gave the door a hefty slam.

As he drank his coffee, he tried in vain to find explanations for Emma's mood — she wasn't overworked and she'd seemed pleased with her recent salary increase.

Mark had always considered himself an easy-going boss but still he had the feeling that her displeasure was directed against him, personally.

Right from the start, they'd established an easy working relationship and soon they'd become good friends, as well as colleagues.

At least, he thought they were friends — sometimes they went out for a meal after work or to a concert, and he'd even thought their relationship might have developed into something more meaningful if things had been different. If it hadn't been for Katie, that was . . .

MARK had been ten years old when Katie had come into his life. She was seven — a skinny little girl with tanned skin, untidy black hair and laughing eyes — when she moved into the cottage next door to Mark's.

Later Mark was to learn from his mildly disapproving mother that the little girl's equally Bohemian-looking parents were both artists.

But all Mark cared about was the scruffy girl with braces on her teeth who could climb the old willow tree quicker than he could. Their cottages stood alone on the outskirts of the village, and Katie's home soon became Mark's second and favourite home.

At the Grants' cottage, no-one cared about the noise levels or noticed the stray kittens and abandoned fox cubs that regularly found their way inside.

As the years passed, Katie and Mark became inseparable.

Mark supposed it was when he left the village to go to university that their friendship turned to love, at least on his part.

Although he met lots of girls there, none of them matched up to the girl who had waited at the station with him, blinking back her tears. None of them was Katie . . .

Mark yearned for the long summer break but when it arrived, nothing was the same. He and Katie were still close but something had changed. It certainly wasn't his love for her . . . He sensed that distance was putting a strain on their relationship and was confident that when he returned to live in the village, everything would be back to normal.

Just before he left university though, Katie dropped her bombshell. "It's one of those once in a lifetime opportunities, Mark," she'd said excitedly. "I've got the chance to go to Canada on a year's exchange!" She'd be home in twelve months, she told him.

What she didn't tell him, and what neither of them could have guessed, was that she would be bringing her Canadian fiancé with her. Katie was marrying someone else!

On her return, she'd still treated Mark like her best friend, telling him her every thought, and chattering on for hours about Peter, the new love in her life. It was bizarre.

Mark was even the first to see the white satin and lace creation that Katie was to wear on her wedding day. All the while his world was crumbling around him.

On the day of the wedding, Mark stood in the small village church with his hands clenched behind his back, mentally reciting every song he'd ever learnt and every piece of poetry — anything to blot out the sound of their voices, most of all her voice, as she said softly, "I do."

THE door to his office opened and Mark looked up, dazed. He was so wrapped up in his memories, that he half-expected to see Katie walking towards him. But it wasn't Katie who entered the room carrying a neat pile of letters to be signed. It was Emma.

Mark hid his disappointment behind a falsely-bright smile. He forced himself to be sociable.

"Any plans for the weekend, Emma?"

"No plans," Emma replied. "You?" Mark was taken aback by the cool tone of her voice.

"Not really." Yet, as he spoke, he knew what he had to do and his heart started to race in anticipation.

"Something's come up, Emma. I'll have to leave the office now. You'll lock up, won't you?"

If anything, she seemed even more curt than she had earlier.

"Naturally."

"Thanks." Mark signed the letters without checking them and, with a brief smile, handed them back to Emma. Then he grabbed his jacket and followed her into the outer office. "See you Monday then, Emma. Have a good weekend."

As he left the office, Mark cringed at the almighty bang he heard just after he closed the door.

It sounded as if Emma had started throwing things but that was ridiculous.

And he didn't have time to go back to investigate. After nine long years, he was finally going to see Katie again.

S HE'S back," Mark's mother had told him a few months ago. Katie was not only back in the country but she was back in the village.

Peter, Mark was told, had managed to get a job with the aerospace company based nearby and two of the three children — yes, three — were now at the same village school that their mother had attended.

Peter was successful but then so was Mark now.

In an attempt to ease the pain, he had tried the age-old trick of burying himself in work. He now had his own flourishing business and, though the pain had dulled to an ache, it was still there.

Now, as he drove, Mark remembered those long, golden days of childhood. In his mind's eye, he could see Katie running across Arrow Hill with the wind in her hair. He could almost hear her calling, "Wait for me, Mark."

And Mark had been waiting for her ever since.

He parked his car outside his parents' cottage, glad they were out, and walked towards the village, deliberately taking the long route past the old brick house that Katie and her husband now owned, promising himself it would be "just once" . . . but he had to see her again, he had to . . .

Playing in the garden was a child, no more than three years old, and her long, black hair reminded him so much of Katie that it was almost unbearable to watch. The child turned and spotted him. "Hello. Who are you?"

Mark laughed softly, remembering. No child of Katie's could ever be shy.

Before he could answer, Mark heard his name being called and then Katie was running across the lawn towards him.

She was laughing, and her long hair was flying behind her.

"Mark! What a lovely surprise." She threw her arms around his neck and hugged him. "What are you doing here?"

Katie was in his arms again, where she belonged, and Mark was too overcome to think straight.

"Oh, Mark," Katie laughed, in sheer delight. "It's been so long! I haven't seen you for years."

He wanted to hold her forever; to savour those precious moments . . . She was exactly the same.

Well almost . . . She was nine years older, of course, and a wife and mother instead of the young girl he remembered.

"Peter," Katie called out. "Peter, look who's here!"

Mark's heart lurched. He hadn't reckoned on Peter being at home.

Peter came outside, smiling indulgently at his excited wife. After the social niceties, the three of them walked into the house, Katie in the middle with her arms linked through theirs. "I've so much to tell you, Mark!"

Katie talked and Mark watched and listened. She was so happy with her life. She had no idea that Mark had spent the last nine years longing for her so much it almost tore him apart. She still regarded him as her best friend.

Suddenly she jumped up. "Won't be a minute. I've got a cake in the oven for Gemma's birthday. I don't want to burn it."

Peter was easy enough to talk to, which was just as well because Mark couldn't concentrate.

Slowly, it began to sink in that this man was Katie's husband. This was the man she had chosen to spend the rest of her life with and the man she had chosen to be the father of her children. He and Katie were a couple, and it was easy to see that they were very much in love.

Katie returned from the kitchen grinning widely. "Just caught it in time! Now — what have you been up to, Mark? How's the business doing?"

A S the afternoon passed pleasantly, Mark found his thoughts straying to what had prompted Emma's strange mood that morning. He should have put more effort into finding out.

Perhaps she hadn't felt well, or perhaps one of her parents had been taken ill. Whatever the reason, Mark hoped it wasn't serious. He wasn't sure how he would cope without her. If she really was fed up with working for him and decided to look for a more fulfilling job, he would have to cope without her.

He could find another secretary but he and Emma were friends, and that couldn't be replaced. No, wait a minute, he thought, they were more than friends . . .

Mark wished he could forget Emma and concentrate on Katie. He knew that these brief hours with her would have to last him for a long time. But at the back of his mind, he knew that this was a different Katie.

That Katie that he'd longed for during the last nine years was a fun-loving girl, and this Katie, who was so thrilled to see her old chum, was a warm, caring adult.

Somewhere in his mind lurked the truth but it was too painful to face at the moment.

With invitations to "come again soon" ringing in his ears, Mark took his leave.

Once out of sight, Mark ran all the way to Arrow Hill, not stopping until he reached the top. Emotionally drained, he flopped down on the grass and stared at the sprawling village below him.

It was as if something very precious had been lost this afternoon.

Then he scoffed at his own stupidity. A dream couldn't be precious. And that's all it had been, he realised now. Just a dream.

Katie had been so much more mature than he had, knowing instinctively that their relationship couldn't develop into true love.

When Mark reached his parents' cottage, his mother met him in the garden. Her expression of pleasure and surprise quickly turned to anxiety.

"You've seen her, haven't you?"

Mark nodded.

"I've just come from there." He squeezed his mother's shoulder to reassure her. "It's OK, Mum. Everything's fine."

"Such lovely children," his mother said, searching his face. "And Katie's such a good mother."

Mark realised his mother was worrying about separations and divorces, and he smiled.

"Yes. They're a very happy family. I'm pleased for them.

"Katie was making a cake for young Gemma. It's her birthday tomorrow and —" Mark stopped abruptly. "Her birthday," he murmured to himself.

"Mark? What is it?"

Mark glanced at his watch. "Sorry, Mum, but I've got to dash."

"You're not staying tonight?" his mother called out, but Mark was already heading for his car with the keys in his hand.

When at last Mark reached the office, Emma had already left. He gave a rueful laugh at the sight that met him.

His desk was hidden beneath the contents of two wastepaper baskets and on top of this mountain of scrap was a white envelope with his name neatly typed on it. Still smiling, he put the envelope in his pocket and left. He drove straight to Emma's flat.

WHEN she opened the door to him, her surprise was evident and colour rushed to her cheeks.

"You — you'd better come in, Mark."

They stood in her living-room, facing each other.

"Happy birthday, Emma," Mark said quietly.

He couldn't understand how he had forgotten. They had hired a boat on her last birthday. It had been a good day, a day when Mark had hoped their relationship would progress to something more.

But it hadn't progressed and now Mark saw the reason for that. He had shut Emma out. Because her name wasn't Katie and because she couldn't fill his head with happy childhood memories, he'd shut her out.

"I thought you'd forgotten," Emma said awkwardly.

Mark knew now that was the explanation for her strange mood. She hadn't been angry, just hurt. Guilty as he felt about that, it touched him to know that she cared.

"I had forgotten," he admitted. "I'm sorry." It wasn't the right time to tell her about Katie so he said instead, "I went to see an old friend today and there was mention of a birthday in the family."

"And this old friend —" Emma asked, eyes on the carpet "— was she pleased to see you?"

Her eyes jerked upwards, just in time to see the surprise on Mark's face. But Emma knew him well, Mark realised — and she cared. She had cared about him for so long, which was why he had hurt her so deeply.

"Yes." Mark reached for her hand and felt it tremble in his own. "I hadn't seen her since her wedding. Tomorrow, I'll tell you about Katie but today it's your birthday and I'm taking you out to celebrate.

"Oh, and this —" He released her hand and reached inside his pocket for the white envelope, "this was on my desk."

Emma's complexion turned an even brighter shade of pink and she grabbed the envelope. "Hey, that's my resig — you've been back to the office!"

"Put it through the shredder on Monday," Mark suggested. "Let's forget work tonight."

"Yes, let's!" Emma agreed, eyes shining with unexpected happiness.

Mark knew he had spent so long hankering after a dream that, even when the truth had been placed in front of him, he hadn't seen it.

But Emma had known and she had waited for him. He held out his hand and Emma slipped her hand into his.

"Let's go and celebrate," Mark said softly.

And they both knew that they were celebrating much more than a birthday. ■

ESCAPE

There are times in a life
When you need a break.
Days full of strife
Are hard to take.
Take a deep breath and cross the floor.
Put on your coat and shut the door.
Take train, coach or car,
Escape the street,
Out into the country and on to your feet.
A loitering stroll down a leafy lane,
Sunshine and shadows, bright sky or rain,
A field, a river, and clumps of trees.
A small bird singing. Just give me these.
I'll return refreshed to the constant strife
That is, for most of us, daily life.
Whenever I lie on a bed of pain
I close my eyes and I dream again
Of wide blue skies and purple moors,
Of soaring hills and sandy shores,
I flee from the mess that man has made
To the God-given peace of a leafy glade.

*A poem by Joyce Stranger, inspired by
an illustration by Mark Viney.*

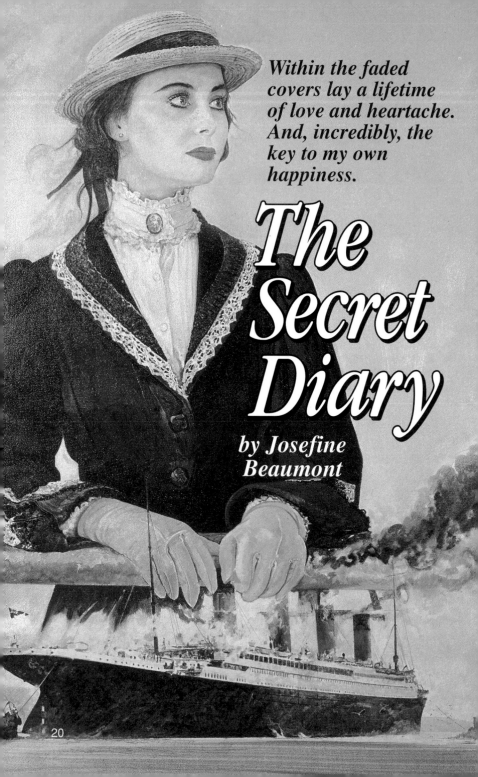

Within the faded
covers lay a lifetime
of love and heartache.
And, incredibly, the
key to my own
happiness.

The Secret Diary

by Josefine Beaumont

20

THIS is my day, the day of my dreams, the culmination of all my hopes. There was a time when I thought that this day would never come. I didn't think that the problems that faced me could ever be resolved.

And yet here I am, calm, filled with an inner peace, a quiet happiness that blankets me in a glow of warmth.

All dressed now, just waiting . . .

My eyes turn to the faded diary and I reach for it, clasp it to my heart, and I remember . . .

No-one ever knew exactly how old Great-Aunt Delia was. All we knew was that she was very old and that we all loved her dearly . . . me especially.

She'd always been there in my life, spoiling me terribly, something I could well have done without, for I was rather wilful as a child.

"Mum says she can't do a thing with me!" I once informed Aunt Delia with great pride and relish, and a look of amusement spread across her wrinkled face.

"Is that a fact?" she murmured and I nodded vigorously.

"Well then, dear," she said in that practical way of hers, "perhaps she shouldn't try!" and I beamed with pleasure.

Dee, as I was allowed to call her, lived in a quaint cottage that sat on the edge of the village and which was overshadowed by a small copse. Her house was a conglomeration of things she had accumulated over many years.

It was wonderful, a real treasure-trove . . . and every item of her collection held its own fascinating story.

Oh, I wish you had known her! We always had such good times together.

I see myself, maybe eight years old, sitting on the riverbank, with my legs dangling in the water, and a tiddler jar tied to my big toe by a piece of string — Dee's idea, and a good one, too.

But then Dee was full of good ideas . . . and she wasn't above dangling her own legs in the water, especially on a hot day.

"Bliss!" she'd cry with a grin.

And as for her picnic hampers! They were always packed with good things. Home cured ham, glazed with honey, dotted with cloves. Hot fresh bread into which butter would run in thick rivulets. Jam tarts overflowing with jam and it didn't matter how many I ate as far as Dee was concerned.

"Food's to be enjoyed, dear," she would state, and I didn't disagree. I loved her spirit of fun, and the freedom I felt with her.

But although there was laughter, there were sad times, too.

I was nine years old when Dee's Labrador dog died. It was my first taste of death and I was devastated.

"He was very old and tired, dear," Dee told me, masking her own grief for my sake, though I didn't realise that at the time.

"And you mustn't cry so. He wouldn't want you to be unhappy. He loved you as much as you loved him."

Raising my tear-stained face to hers, I suddenly realised how very old my darling Dee was. Her face was a criss-cross, a cobweb of lines and creases, her bright blue eyes faded.

And with fear, and the candour of youth, I blurted out, "You're very old, aren't you, Dee?" I held my breath for her reply.

It seemed an age in coming for she hesitated before saying gently, "Oh, very old, dear."

"You, you . . ." I swallowed hard. "You won't die, will you? Will you?"

"One day, I will." She smiled brightly. "When my time comes.

"But this is your time for being young and happy, for growing and changing and learning all about this wonderful world we live in. You don't need to worry about death."

"Promise me that you'll live for years and years!" I threw myself into her arms in a sudden burst of emotion. "Promise!"

And she held me against her lilac-scented chest and said gently, "My dear child, I have every intention of living to be a hundred so that I can receive my telegram from the Queen.

"But, apart from that, I promise," she held me at arms' length, eyes moist with love, "to live long enough to see you full-grown and settled."

I'll say one thing for my dear, darling Dee. She kept her promise.

DEE saw me through the difficult years of adolescence, always prepared to listen, and to talk.

And though it seemed odd that I should ask a woman who had never married, I once asked her, "How will I know when I'm in love?"

A beautiful look flittered across her face before she replied quietly, "Oh, my darling, you will know, believe me."

And she was right.

When I did fall in love, however, I faced bitter opposition from my parents.

In the end I turned to the one person whom I knew could offer me love and understanding without condemnation.

★ ★ ★ ★

Dee and I sat in her parlour one evening, a tray of tea between us.

"I don't know what to do, Dee," I said dully. "Tell me what to do." I was worn out by the arguments and tears and bitter recriminations.

"Only you can know that, dear," she said quietly. "But . . . well, I'd like you to have this . . ."

She rose and unlocked the bureau, taking out a faded, leather-bound book.

For a moment she held it to her, eyes closed, stiff hands stroking the cover and then, drawing a breath, she handed me the book.

"This was to be yours, one day. Because you were the daughter I never had, and because I love you, but more importantly still, because knowing me as you do I felt that you, of all people, would understand where others wouldn't. Read it and then . . . well, the rest is up to you."

She made her slow way from the room, closing the door silently behind her.

It was her diary. For a moment I hesitated. A diary is a private thing, the secret person in all of us. There, words are written from the heart, meant only for the eyes of the author.

And then, feeling a sense of love that defies description, I curled my legs under me, settled into the chair and began to read.

THIS was a Delia I had never known. The 11-year-old child, sailing to India with her mother and father, who was a major in the Indian army.

Through her wonderfully descriptive narrative, I saw the ship sail into the heat and clamour and colour of Bombay, under an azure-blue sky.

I rode with her on the train to Delhi and I came to know the house with its verandah and flowering jasmine where she was to spend the next 15 years.

The people in her life came alive for me. The ayah who looked after her, the gentle servants whom she grew to love, the army families with whom they socialised.

Her words took me to the soirées, the polo matches, the balls where the ladies wore chiffon and silk and jewels in their hair.

I travelled with her through those growing years, and I was with her the evening she met Rajit.

I shared those stolen hours she spent with him in Kashmir, and I watched her as she sailed with him on the Dal Lake where he first kissed her.

I saw her walking hand in hand with him through the wooded hills of Simla on yet another secret meeting and I knew that I would never again hear the soft rustle of the breeze whisper through the trees without remembering two people who had lived and loved all those years ago in that jewel of a country.

The shadows had lengthened in the room and tears had stained my face before I finally closed the book.

I REMEMBER when Mahatma Ghandi came to Delhi," Dee told me that night.

"Such a little, insignificant man and yet, a man of dreams. They called him the Peaceful One," she mused.

"He had a massive following and he was welcomed in Delhi with all the pomp and ceremony that the British Raj could muster.

"But you know, dear," she continued, "there was an undercurrent. One could feel it tangibly. There was a deep feeling of injustice between the many conflicting beliefs — Muslims, Hindus, Sikhs.

"Nobody wanted trouble, for people remembered only too well how the streets of Amritsar had run with blood," she said sadly, "but still, news filtered in from Jaipur and there was gossip in the bazaars of fires and killings.

"Then, one night, the trouble came to a head. We had to bolt the doors, as the servants had deserted us. My parents were distraught.

"All I could think was that Ghandi's dream had been an impossible one . . . as had mine.

"Rajit and I knew we could never marry. We'd accepted that. His future was all mapped out. His bride had been chosen when they were both children.

"And after all, mixed marriages were totally unacceptable. We knew that and we were prepared.

"We loved each other and that was all that mattered.

"Our dream ended that night. With the first light, my parents and I were escorted under an army guard to Bombay and we set sail that same evening.

"I watched the bay recede and something in me died because, under all that gentleness and beauty, had lain anger and hatred. And though I have lived a long life, I left my heart in Delhi with my Rajit and all that was left to me were memories to live on."

She fell silent and our hands met as did our eyes.

"Thank you, Dee," I breathed, and she smiled and asked softly, "What will you do, dear?"

"Oh, Dee!" I clung to her, rocked her to me before replying firmly, "I will follow my heart!"

And she smiled.

WHEN I arrived home my parents were watching TV. "Hello, love." Dad smiled at me and I kissed the top of his head in response. Then, turning to my mother I said, "We have to talk, Mum."

"We have talked!" she protested stiffly and I shook my head and replied, "No, Mum, we haven't. We've argued, that's what we've done, and I can't stand it. It's tearing me in two. I love you, I love you both. I don't want us to argue any more."

I saw her exchange a look with Dad. I saw her bottom lip tremble before she said, "I wish you'd never met him, Laura."

"But I did meet him," I said gently. "And I love him, Mum. We want a life together, children. Please don't deny me that. Please don't ask me to choose."

"Is that what you think I'm doing?" She stared at me and I stared back and said, "Well, isn't it?"

"She's right, Mary." Dad patted her hand and I threw him a grateful look.

"We'll lose her, Henry!" Mum started to cry. "She'll be halfway across the world and we'll never see her again!"

Dad smiled. "Aeroplanes do fly to Australia, you know, Mary. We'll be able to go there on holiday!"

Mum sniffed, looking happier.

I asked timidly, "Can I phone him, Mum? Will you let him come over?"

"No, you won't phone him!" she snapped, making my heart sink, but then, getting up, she added, "I'll phone and invite him to supper. I might as well get to know him . . . though, if you ask me, it won't last, holiday romances never do . . . why you had to go and fall for an Aussie I'll never know.

"What's wrong with British lads, anyway?" she continued. "You were always wilful, though. I never could do a thing with you . . ." Her voice trailed away as she marched into the hall to phone.

Dad and I smiled at each other in relief.

"Ready?" Dad's voice jerked me back into the present and I turned to face him. His features suffused with pride as he said gruffly, "You look beautiful, lass."

"Oh, Dad!" I grinned, going into his arms and he patted me and said, "None of that, none of that, else I'll start crying . . . fine fool that'd make me look!"

"I love you," I sniffed.

"I love you, too, lass."

He beamed and, laughing, we went out into the sunshine where the neighbours were waiting for a glimpse of us.

I heard the oohs and aahs and Dad's chest puffed out as he boasted, "I feel like a film star, lass!"

"It's me they're looking at, Dad," I reminded him.

"Rubbish!" he snorted. "Who'd spare you a look when there's a handsome fellow like me to ogle over?" and I giggled.

"It was a wonderful wedding present Dee gave you both," Dad said, and my eyes filled with tears. Wonderful indeed.

I thought of the envelope containing the air tickets and hotel bookings that she had given us. It was her last gift to me. It is one I shall treasure . . .

For I, too, will sail upon the Dal Lake with my love in the Vale of Kashmir. I, too, will walk hand in hand with my love through the hills of Simla.

I looked down at my hands. I carried no flowers, not even a prayer book. Instead, decorated by a silken gold cross that was fastened by a silk ribbon, I had chosen Dee's diary.

"I wish she had lived to see this day, lass, she'd have been fit to burst." Dad patted my hand. "I wish she could be here with you."

"She is, Dad," I breathed gently. "Oh, she is . . ." ■

*He wanted so much
to come home —
and she was the
only one who
could help him
do that . . .*

The Final
Homecoming

by Sara Jane MacDonald

FERGUS stood on the top deck of the ferry, looking ahead to where the island of Arran would appear in the grey sea of dawn. As the peaks of Goat Fell loomed out of the mist, he felt as if he had never been away.

How could he have stayed away so long? How could he have forgotten the beauty of this place where he was born?

He disembarked slowly, a tall man with a tired, sun-tanned face, arriving unannounced.

He walked away from the docks, his rucksack on his back, feeling instinctively the slower pace of the island, as he began the long walk uphill out of Brodick.

He breathed deeply, taking in the scent of heather and sea and the faint fragrance of wild flowers.

He knew Iona would not be where he had last left her but he wanted to retrace his steps, go back to the point of his leaving, so that he would know how to move forward.

He shuddered as he thought of his behaviour and remembered the pain, glittering like splinters of bright glass, behind her eyes.

Most people had to leave to find work on the mainland and he had been no exception — except that he had been too easily seduced by the bright lights and a pretty face.

"I'm sorry," he had announced suddenly and abruptly. "I love someone else. We're leaving for New York next week."

He had avoided looking at her slim hand, which had worn his ring since she was 16.

He was drawing near her house and his heart beat faster, although he knew she would probably be somewhere else now.

Everything was silent as he approached. He saw that her house was unlived in — a summer place waiting for the ferrylanders.

He felt a stab of disappointment as he stood looking at the shuttered house. Echoes of long-gone voices haunted him with wasted chances.

He sat on the wall, tucking himself in under the weeping tree, letting the memories wash over him in gentle waves.

Perhaps he slept? Perhaps he was dreaming? For he heard the sudden sounds of singing, a dog barking, dim voices.

Shutters on the closed windows were thrown back, windows gaped wide and the house looked at him with open eyes.

Someone was singing; a child's voice called out with laughter and an old dog ran, ears flapping, finding him where he sat hidden by the tree.

The dog did not bark and a woman watching from the window saw the tail wagging near the flowering tree, yet saw nothing but shadows.

She came down into the garden with the child and moved towards the tree, calling the dog.

They saw the man and stopped. The woman drew in her breath, her eyes flying to his face.

Fergus held her eyes steadily, remembering the young girl of yesterday who always found his boyhood hiding place, helped by her dog.

The child holding the straining animal was puzzled by the stillness of his mother and this man, and called his mother's name.

The moment broken, Fergus turned to look at the boy — and he knew!

This boy was not just familiar, this boy was his!

His mind flew across a continent to a failed relationship and a woman who, after all, had not been carrying his child.

His dreams had died — and it was Iona who had carried his child, who had coped alone.

The woman in the garden, watching his slumped back, for a moment forgot the hard years and the sadness and saw only the lost child in the man she loved.

Behind him, she saw frail cobwebs, still glistening with dew, caught on the tree behind his head.

It seemed to her, love was as frail as those intricate woven circles — so easily broken by a careless hand.

And, yet, if a strand broke, the spider diligently set about weaving another. He never gave up.

All these years, had she not been weaving the strand between them until this moment when he reached her?

Fergus wondered how he could ever have left her.

But, as she smiled, he realised he never had. She had been travelling with him, here in his heart, guiding him homewards.

Iona and small Fergus stand by the tree shimmering with summer cobwebs.

There is no-one there and now the old dog whines and comes to lie at their feet.

Iona sees there are no footprints on the grass and a feeling of such sadness and loss fill's her being.

She knows the dog found his old hiding place. She knows Fergus stood beside them on the lawn a moment ago. She knows it!

Someone is calling, crying and calling her name. She runs awkwardly towards the sounds.

Fergus's mother looks ashen. "Fergus was coming home," she cries out. "He was on his way home to us, when his car hit a . . . Oh, Iona, he never made it home."

Iona walks back to the tree and gently touches the fragile cobwebs.

"Oh, yes, he did," she whispers. "He made it home." ■

From This Moment On...

by Jane O'Hare

**It was a time for looking forward, not back — yet
he couldn't help remembering another radiant
bride from days long ago . . .**

STOP worrying, Jackie," Bill said quietly, drawing his daughter's arm
through his, and enfolding her cool fingers in his own. "Your car's only
three minutes overdue, the bridesmaids will only just have arrived at
Saint Mary's, so don't fret."

His hazel eyes crinkled as he smiled down at her, and he wished he could
see her face, but it was hidden beneath the full, shadowing veil.

Bill's heart was filled with a mixture of tenderness and awe and he swallowed to ease the lump in his throat. If only Vera could see her now.

Jackie's head was inclined away from him as they waited in the quiet hallway. She seemed to be watching the pale November sunlight as it glowed through the panes of coloured glass in the front door.

She didn't speak, and he wondered what she was thinking while they waited together at the start of her journey into a new life.

Were her clear hazel eyes — so like his own — gazing into her future as Tim's wife, or was she remembering the sadness of last year?

Perhaps she was thinking, as he was, just how momentous the walk down the aisle on his arm would be. Her final short journey as a single girl.

Life, Bill thought, was like a series of journeys. You were always going from one place to another — saying hello . . . or goodbye.

Vera's face shimmered into his mind and his heart stumbled, but today of all days he mustn't allow it to sink low. Vera would not have wanted that.

She'd have been overjoyed for Jackie and Tim, would have revelled in each moment of the past weeks of preparation. And she would have been waiting with tears of happiness in her eyes and on her cheeks, for him to take his place in the pew next to her when he'd given their beloved daughter away.

"How late is it now, Dad?" Jackie asked.

"Just about five minutes, love, that's all," he reassured her after a glance at his watch. "Sure you don't want to sit down in the living-room?"

"I'm too edgy to sit down, Dad," she said. "Besides, it should be here any minute now."

Bill nodded. Looking at his daughter in all her splendour made him too emotional to trust his voice.

The white gleam of her dress appeared translucent through the veiling which reached her waist. He could see, too, how her soft dark hair shone beneath its crown of veiling and orange-blossom.

Her bouquet rested on the table beside the hall mirror. A beautiful shower of roses.

Vera had had a gift for handling flowers, and Jackie would have wanted her to make the bouquet — she'd said so. They hadn't been able to use lily of the valley, though — Vera's own favourite — because it was the wrong time of the year.

IT had been the wrong time of the year for them when Jackie had made her very first journey into the world. Two days before Christmas, 23 years ago.

There'd been a cold snap and snow had been falling heavily as he'd driven Vera to hospital — and still falling hours later when he'd at last been allowed to see her, and their baby.

Bill could still remember, quite clearly, the picture his wife and daughter had presented on that wonderful day.

"She's the living image of you, Bill," Vera had said when he'd bent to kiss her and take his first peep at the wrapped bundle in her arms.

Yes, even he had been able to see that the crinkle-faced infant had eyes the same shape as his, the same shaped ears, too.

"She won't be a plain Jane like me." Vera had smiled contentedly. "But good-looking, like her dad."

Dear Vera. She'd never been plain to him. There was such beauty inside her that it glowed through what she'd always referred to as her ordinary features, and the hair she'd dismissed as mousey had always felt as soft as down to his fingers.

He'd wanted to take her her favourite lilies of the valley after the birth, but there'd only been hothouse blooms in the shops. Then, walking back to his car empty-handed, he'd seen the solution in a display window of a clothes shop.

IT was a hat with a bunch of imitation lily of the valley gracing its crown. Vera never wore hats, and it was shatteringly expensive, but he'd bought it and removed the silk flowers to take to her.

Her face had glowed and her eyes had glimmered with tears when he'd presented them to her. "Oh Bill, I'll treasure them for always," she'd said.

And she had. She'd worn them as a spray on her dress for special occasions, such as Jackie's christening, on the few evenings they'd gone out for a meal together, and at friends' weddings.

Over the years their whiteness had faded to dusty cream and the deep green leaf had become yellowed. But Vera had covered them with film to protect them, and kept them in a Dresden vase on the mantelshelf.

They'd been the first thing his eyes had fallen on after Vera's last journey. Unable to bear it, he'd taken them down and, to Jackie's horror, crushed them out of sight in a drawer.

"I think the car's come, Dad," Jackie said, breaking into his thoughts, and he opened the front door.

There was a group of neighbours waiting near the gate and he heard little gasps of admiration for his daughter as he led her to the glittering Daimler.

There were calls of, "Good luck, Jackie — all the best." And then the car was pulling away from the kerb, transporting them on to the next stage of Jackie's special journey.

"Are you all right, lass?" His voice was gravelly with feeling as he looked at her, holding her bouquet, silent and beautiful beside him.

"Yes, Dad," she said, but her voice quivered, and he put his hand on her wrist and squeezed it reassuringly.

It had been Vera who'd been with Jackie on her earliest first journeys. The day she'd taken her very first steps, Vera had proudly told him all about it, when he'd got home from work.

Before long, their daughter was walking, then running, everywhere.

The years had flown and soon she was making that first journey to school. Vera had shared her mixed feelings with her husband that evening.

"She looked so tiny, Bill, so vulnerable, walking away from me. She didn't cry — but I did, coming home alone afterwards."

Thirteen years later, Jackie was off on another important journey to teacher training college. Oh, how they'd missed her, and how proud he'd felt collecting her at the station on end-of-term holidays.

But there'd been other first journeys for Jackie to face alone.

He remembered her first interview for a post as teacher and the first day she'd been accepted.

Then, at the beginning of last year, Vera . . .

That had been a sad and terrible journey he and Jackie had shared that day. He forced his thoughts away from it, back to Jackie.

She'd met Tim on the plane on the way to Turkey last year. It had been her first break after losing her mother.

Meeting Tim had been the start of the most important journey of her life so far . . .

THEY'D arrived. The car was drawing up at the open gates leading to the church. Saint Mary's, where he and Vera had married, where Jackie had been christened, and where Vera . . .

Bill's thoughts ended as he walked round to the other side of the car, to where Jackie was getting out, and helped her from the car.

There were people standing at the gates, and others lining the path to the church doors, where the bridesmaids waited, the skirts of their lemon dresses fluttering in the November breeze.

The watery sun made Jackie's dress shine and shimmer, and a murmur of delight came from the friends and well-wishers lining the way.

Bill glanced down at his daughter beside him and a searing bolt of pride and love shot through him.

Then they were gathered with the bridesmaids in the porch. There were whispers and adjustments being made, a pressure on his arm from Jackie, and, as they stepped forward together, the chords of the wedding march began.

Filled with emotion, he led his daughter reverently up the aisle to where Tim waited, best man at his side, eyes glowing darkly in his handsome face.

And then that last, brief journey was ended. There were rustlings, a cough, and Bill heard the words, "Who giveth this woman in Holy Matrimony?"

It was time to perform his last fatherly duty.

The service moved on. Jacqueline Rosemary and Timothy Mark became man and wife and the ring was placed on her finger.

In the vestry, Jackie signed her maiden name for the last time. Now Bill was on his own . . .

THERE was laughter around him, returning him to the moment. And suddenly, there was Jackie, the new ring gleaming on her finger, putting her hand on his arm, and saying quietly, "Thank you, Dad . . . for today and everything."

The veil was thrown back from her face, her radiant, beautiful face, and her thickly-lashed blue eyes met his own. The smile she gave him was so similar to his own.

There was nothing of Vera about her . . .

And then he saw it, fastened on the bodice of her shining white wedding gown.

The creamy, slightly crushed spray of lily of the valley. Vera's spray, which he'd thought he would never be able to look at again.

He braced himself, but the expected pain didn't come. Instead, it was as if all the hurt he had kept bottled up inside him in a tight knot of grief, was finally ebbing away.

When he lifted his eyes to meet Jackie's, shining with the magic of the day, he thought happily, Vera was here. She is here in Jackie's heart always, just as she is in mine.

They held each others' gaze, father and daughter, and he knew how perfectly she understood his feelings, just as Vera always had.

That was how Jackie was, and always would be, like her mother; a woman of loving understanding.

Tim came to her now, and she linked her arm in his for her first journey as a wife. Following the bridesmaids, Bill's heart was filled with peace. The future no longer seemed so bleak nor so lonely.

His thoughts were turned ahead, to a day when there'd be another child, or children, who would take first journeys, too. And perhaps they, too, would hold his hand, just as their mother had done . . . ■

TWO TO SEW

You'll love our two delightful cross-stitch projects.

Christmas Treat Gift Bag

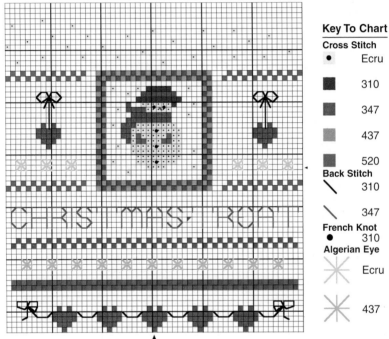

Key To Chart

Cross Stitch
- ●   Ecru
- ■   310
- ■   347
- ■   437
- ■   520

Back Stitch
- ＼   310
- ＼   347

French Knot
- ●   310

Algerian Eye
- ✳   Ecru
- ✳   437

This bag would make a gift extra special. It could also be filled with sweets or pot-pourri and hung on the tree.

- ◆ **Two 14 x 10 in (36.5 x 26.5 cm) pieces of 32 count Belfast linen in natural**
- ◆ **Size 26 tapestry needle**
- ◆ **DMC stranded cotton as listed in the key**
- ◆ **1 yd (1 m) of ¼ in (5 mm) red ribbon**

- ◆ **Gold bells or other Christmas decoration trimmings**

1 Fold the first piece of linen in half vertically to find the middle, measure 2½ in (6 cm) up from the bottom, find the centre stitch on the fold and begin work here.

2 Stitch the design from the chart using two strands of DMC stranded cotton for the cross stitch, French knots and the Algerian eye stitch (see stitch diagram) and one strand for the backstitch.

3 When the stitching is complete, count thirty-seven threads from the top stitching row and withdraw four threads. This is to thread the ribbon through. Count twenty threads further up again and withdraw three threads. Using antique hem stitch (see stitch diagram), make a hem using one strand of red stranded cotton.

4 Take the second piece of fabric (the back of the bag), and withdraw four threads as for the ribbon row and three threads for the hemming, to match the front of the bag.

5 With right sides together sew up the sides and bottom. Press the seams and clip the corners. Turn the bag the right way out and thread the ribbon through the withdrawn row. Add the bells and pull up and tie.

You can order
THE NEW CROSS
STITCH SAMPLER
BOOK for the special
price of £10.99 (rrp £11.99)
plus FREE p&p (UK mainland only).
To order, please call the David & Charles
Credit card Hotline on 01626 334555 and
quote code Z792.

Gather The Flowers Sampler

This small sampler will look lovely as a picture. The design would also look good made up as a pincushion.

<table>
<tr><td colspan="2" align="center">Finished size: 4¼ x 4 in
(11 x 10 cm) Stitch count: 59 x 57</td></tr>
</table>

◆ **8 in (20 cm) square of 32 count Belfast linen in raw linen**
◆ **DMC stranded cotton as listed in the key**
◆ **Size 26 tapestry needle**

Key To Chart

Cross Stitch

●	Ecru			726
■	310		■	814
■	369		■	3609
■	437		■	3746
■	502		■	3768

Back Stitch

\	310
\	433
\	502
\	3746
\	3768

Algerian Eye Stitch

This pretty star-shaped stitch can be used with cross stitch to great effect. It generally occupies the space of two cross stitches and is worked in such a way that an evenly shaped, almost square stitch is produced with a small hole formed in the centre.

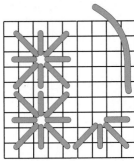

Algerian Eye Stitch

Antique Hemstitch

Algerian Eye Stitch

To work this stitch, decide where the edge of the hem will come and withdraw two or three threads along the length of the piece. Fold the hem so that the turned-under edge just touches the drawn threads and tack in place. Beginning at the left-hand end of the wrong side, bring the thread through from inside the hem, emerging on the wrong side three threads down from the drawn area. Move the needle two threads to the right and surround four of the threads (see diagram). Bring the needle back to the right of the clump of threads and insert it between the hem and the front of the fabric, emerging two threads to the right, ready to take another stitch. Pull the thread tight enough to pull the group of threads together, then repeat.

❶ Find the centre of the fabric and begin stitching here over two threads of linen following the chart, using two strands of stranded cotton for the cross stitch, two strands for the backstitch lettering and one strand for the outlining. Use a hoop to keep the work taut if you wish.

❷ Press the work carefully, and frame.

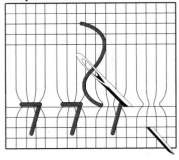

Antique Hemstitch

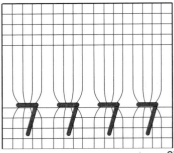

MY LITTLE STRAY CAT

I saw him first one winter day.
His uncaring folks had moved away
And left him behind to make his way,
Catching mice and birds, and be a stray.
I tried to feed him. He'd not come near.
The sight of me produced great fear.
It was cold at night, the frost was keen.
While he froze in the cold, I felt so mean.
I opened up the garden shed.
I put inside it a cosy bed.
A cardboard box with a soft white fleece.
There he could shelter and find some peace.
He ate the food that I put for him there,
But no way would he come indoors for his fare.
His coat now thick, his ear was healed.
He hunted by day in the nearby field.
When the sun was bright he basked on the shelf,
Surrounded by tools and a garden elf.
Then came a night of torrential rain.
Lightning flashed and it thundered,
Again and again.
I heard a scratching on my kitchen door,
Made by a little frantic paw.
I opened the door and in he came,
Away from the crashes and pouring rain.
I put down food and he looked at me,
Then began to feed, though reluctantly.
I left him on a chair and I went to bed.
I woke in the morning and there by my head
Was a tabby cat with shining fur,
A tongue that licked me and a rousing purr.
My little stray has come to stay
And how he brightens my lonely day.

A poem by Joyce Stranger, inspired by an
illustration by Mark Viney.

BOTTOM OF THE CLASS

by Adeline Summers

What a dunce! In trying to make Mum happy, I'd only succeeded in making myself miserable!

I CAME home early and saw at once that my mother had been crying. She turned away, but I saw her red eyes and the bits of straight hair that were wet with tears.

I was almost at my wits' end. This was the third time in as many months, and having a mother to look after wasn't easy for a 12-year-old boy.

Dad had been gone for over 18 months now, and I had got over the upset, but it looked as though Mum never would.

I remember the morning when they both stood together in the kitchen. It was our fry-up morning and all the food was on the table, getting cold.

"Your father's not going to live with us any more, Terry," Mum had said in a flat sort of way. "He still loves us, of course, but he's going to stay somewhere else."

I could tell she didn't believe a word of it, and neither did I — about the still loving us, I mean.

No-one could love you and not want to live in the same house. It didn't make sense.

Mum was surprisingly jolly for the first two weeks. There were lots of outings and treats, but it didn't feel right.

I used to see her looking at me sometimes and it made me feel kind of funny. I could tell she worried about me.

I'd missed Dad at first just like you'd miss your own bed or your favourite chair in the corner, but let's face it, he wasn't an easy man to be with.

Dad had never gone out with us. He'd always been at work or with his pals and, one way or another, I hadn't seen much of him at all.

Paul Myers' father played football with him, and tickled him until he squealed, and Steve Tonks spent hours with his dad messing about with engines.

My dad was never like that. So often I wished he would take me to a football match. He knew how much I liked the game, but he just didn't seem much interested in football — or in me . . .

Mum eventually got over the "jolly" period and things settled down. We were used to there being just the two of us, so it was no big deal.

THEN the crying started again. Mum got very quiet about the house and started to hug me for no reason at all.

This was a few weeks after my bad time at school, when I'd got into trouble for starting the janitor's tractor mower and backing it into a wall.

Actually I hadn't meant to start it at all. I'd just twiddled with one of the knobs, and it had shot off. Of course, I'd got dragged off to see old Chamber Pot, the Head.

Mr Chambers terrified me. .

It was enough to freeze your blood when he fixed you with his laser eyes. All the kids jumped when he had something to say.

He'd completely floored me at first by accepting my explanation about the tractor. Then he'd droned on about mathematics, effort, commitment, and the need to concentrate. I knew my maths was hopeless. I just couldn't understand the subject and I'd become a fixture in the bottom half of the class.

Mum had to go to see him as well. In fact, she went three times and followed each visit by giving me another lecture. Everybody seemed to be pitching into me and I got more and more stroppy.

What did they all expect? I would have tried harder, but once you got behind it wasn't easy to catch up.

I shouted at Mum a few times, but that only made things worse because then I felt dead guilty. I mean, after all, it wasn't her fault.

That was when the tears had started again.

Suddenly, the reason hit me. She needed someone. That was it; another man.

Not someone like Dad who was never there, but a proper man to take her out and make a fuss of her.

I racked my brains — who did I know? Mr Peebles at the butcher's wasn't married, but he was fat and looked as though he rolled around the floor in his clothes.

I couldn't think of many other men. Even at school there were only two who might be of use; Harry Milton and Ray Coleman.

Mr Milton was a big, jovial man who taught games and ran the theatre group. Always laughing at his own terrible jokes and slapping us boys on the back, he had a short fuse, but fooled around and could be quite good fun.

Mr Coleman, short and round-faced, taught science and maths. I didn't like him because he made fun of me in front of the others. I couldn't stomach the thought of him, so it would have to be Flash Harry.

I felt pleased with myself, but a name was one thing, a workable plan quite another.

I couldn't believe my luck the next Monday. There was a big untidy notice on the board advertising for actors for the drama club's production of "The King and I".

The notice ended: We also require help from parents, in particular a mother to take the part of Anna.

I let the information trickle through my brain. I knew Mum used to sing and act a bit. If she got the part, she would meet Mr Milton at every rehearsal — and, well, you never know . . .

I acted my heart out at home. "Mr Milton is desperate," I said. "There's no-one to play Anna."

"Why tell me?" Mum asked, peeling the potatoes.

"'Cause you'd be exactly right." I was lying through my teeth — for all I knew she might be awful and I would have to change schools out of embarrassment.

"Not only that, I could try for a part as well. I've always wanted to have a go."

It was a dangerous gamble, but it paid off. Mum was quite keen, and at the audition was by far the best for the part.

I saw Chamber Pot at the side of the stage and she actually spoke to him after her turn. I went out the emergency exit and round the back to avoid him.

ON Mum's insistence, I tried for the part of Anna's son and was absolutely delighted not to get it. Instead I was given the minor rôle of a Siamese boy in an enormous coolie hat.

All I had to do was drift about at the right times, and murmur, "Getting to know you." That suited me fine and I could keep an eye on events from under my hat.

It went like magic. Mum never missed a rehearsal and Mr Milton strutted about showing her how he wanted the part played, and holding her hands to set them in the correct positions.

It was a good sign, especially when Mr Milton gave us a lift home a few times as well, and came in for coffee.

I could put two and two together and took mine upstairs out of the way.

But what if he came to stay with us? I knew I wouldn't like that. Maybe my brilliant idea wasn't so brilliant after all . . .

One evening Mum said she had to see someone and Mr Milton would take me home and sit with me until she got in.

I felt awkward. His big smile soon faded and we ended up watching television in glum silence.

"How would you feel if things changed?" he asked suddenly.

"What things?" I asked, knowing very well what he meant.

"Well, your mother's on her own right now, but that might not always be the case. You might have to learn how to share her."

I felt a cold hand clutch my insides. There wasn't going to be a lot of fun with him around, that was for sure, but it was too late now.

Mum came in with her face flushed from the cold air, and I went up to bed.

The musical was an enormous success and I was more proud of Mum than I could tell her. I had made up a bunch of flowers from the few left in our garden and, blushing like a ninny, gave them to Mum.

She put aside the huge bouquet she'd been given by the parent/teacher association and fastened a few of my flowers to the front of her dress.

It was a nice thing to do.

It seemed strange to have it all over, and I hadn't a notion as to what would happen next.

Then the tears started again . . .

I wasn't particularly brave. In fact, I'd run a mile to avoid a fight unless I got dragged in, but this was getting ridiculous.

The next time I found Mum drying her eyes I charged in.

"What is it, Mum? What do you keep crying for? You know Dad isn't coming back."

I'd never spoken to her like that except when we were having a row and I was afraid. I needn't have been.

"I think you're big enough now to talk to properly," she said, then paused. "Do you still think about your father?" she asked.

I didn't have to worry about that one. "No," I said. "He never thought about me. It hurt when he went, but it doesn't upset me any more."

Mum looked relieved, and that made me feel better.

"Perhaps it's time to make another start," she said.

I nodded awkwardly.

A softness crept into her eyes and for a dreadful moment I thought she was going to cry again.

"I've met someone else, Terry, and I think we love one another," she said eventually.

"Oh yes," I said, looking away.

"Until now I'd decided to put it out of my mind."

So that was the reason for the tears . . .

"Why?" I asked.

"If we got married, he would take your father's place."

Married? This was getting beyond me. I hadn't bargained on a marriage-and-forever sort of thing.

I'd thought more of a pal to cheer her up a bit. What had I done?

I must have looked perplexed.

"You all right?"

"I don't know, Mum," I blurted. "Honest, just do it, and stop upsetting yourself."

"Right," she said. "I'll come up to the school tomorrow and we'll settle it then."

THE next day in class I was a bag of nerves and couldn't sit still. It was almost a relief when, that afternoon, Mum came to collect me, and we were making the dreaded trip down the corridor.

I knew Mr Milton had a free period because I had looked on the timetables, but, to my surprise, I was pushed straight past his office.

Now that things were completely out of my hands it was frightening. My thoughts were suddenly interrupted by our arrival at the great oak door with the brass plate, Douglas Chambers M. A., B.A. ed.

"No!" I screamed. "I'm not going in there. It's not fair."

"Not him, Mum — please."

The door started to open and I could see the eyes.

Like I said, I'm not brave and, slipping my mother's grasp, I raced off out of the school like a rabbit chased by dogs. I ran to the park and sat on the swings all afternoon getting more and more depressed.

I'd had one father who had never loved me, and looked all set to have another who made me shake with fright.

The injustice of it all bore down on me and I stayed in the park, unhappy and red-eyed until tea-time when my stomach told me it was time to go home.

I couldn't face Mum, so I sneaked into the house, quietly made some sandwiches and retired to the safety of my bedroom to eat them.

Strangely enough, Mum didn't say anything about my running away — except that she was glad I'd come home. Still, she didn't look very glad, only relieved and sad again.

It was Sunday morning when the front door-bell rang. It was our fry-up morning again, and my mind travelled back to that other morning when Dad had left. It was like a bad dream that wouldn't go away.

My throat went dry and I nearly choked on the food when I saw the grey Granada in the drive. I'd seen that plenty of times before . . .

"Answer it will you, love." Mum obviously knew who it was but she didn't look at me at all.

I was terrified, but I went and opened the door, crouching against the post like a man on the gallows.

I saw the shoes first — soft moccasins. No brogues and no pinstripes. Instead there were light brown trousers and a floppy jumper emblazoned with We are the Champions in Everton colours. He still had a shiny head, though.

"Hello, Terry, is your mother in?" How did he know I had a first name?

He walked straight through to the kitchen, and as he passed he sort of tousled my hair with his hand. I jerked my head away.

"Gosh, you're in the middle of breakfast . . . any toast going? I haven't had a bite to eat yet."

I tried to act normal, but spilled tea all down my trousers and had to go and change them.

When I came down, he said, "I found this at home," and dragged a rumpled comic from his pocket.

I couldn't believe it — at school you got lines for having a comic. I didn't say thank you in case it was a trick.

He didn't stay long.

At school it was just the same as always, but I had a shock one day when I couldn't get out of his way after assembly. I swear he winked at me — honest!

He came again on Thursday soon after school, and talked about going tenpin bowling. I urged Mum to go.

"I'll be OK," I said, desperately anxious to get him outside again.

"Don't you want to come?" he asked.

I was petrified but didn't have the nerve to refuse . . .

As I expected, at the bowling alley nothing went right, and my arms and legs refused to behave themselves.

But, to give old Chamber Pot his due, he was very patient and, even when I kept missing all the pins, said I'd done well for the first time.

This won't last long, I thought.

ON Friday we watched television and he played draughts with me — like an ordinary person. I didn't win, but I got three crowns.

I didn't want to go upstairs to do my homework. I dithered inside, wanting to run and hide, yet fascinated by the way he just sat there in our room when there had really never been anyone but Mum and me before.

Still wary, I perched on the far end of the settee and opened my maths book and folder and tried my best to concentrate.

"How's the maths going?" he enquired.

My hand shook with sudden fright. "It's these equations," I said in a funny little voice which didn't sound like mine. "I don't understand them."

He moved over and rested his arm across my shoulders. I stiffened, but there was a comfort in the pressure.

"Nearly there," he said, as though he was interested. "You want to get rid of minus two. Now, how do you do that?"

"Add it on?" I said hopefully.

"Yes, but you add it to both sides, don't you? Try it now, it will work out."

I got them all right but one, and on the Monday Mr Coleman actually smiled at me.

Mr Chambers was away the next week at a conference or something. In a way it was a relief, yet I couldn't help myself watching the road on Saturday.

He came in, kissed Mum and said to me, "Do you jog?"

"I used to," I ventured suspiciously.

"Then we'll go and get some clobber," he said, and ushered me into the back of his car.

He bought me a fantastic track suit, all blue and white. When I came down with it on, he stood back. "Makes you look like Gazza," he said.

Fancy him saying I looked like Paul Gascoigne. I grinned. I couldn't help it, really I couldn't.

They have been married for three months now. I never believed families could be like this, with everybody being happy together.

I don't get bossed around or anything and often get asked my opinion about things as though what I have to say is important.

Took a lot of getting used to I can tell you, but I soon got over being scared. When we go jogging in the park on a Saturday and I wave to my pals, I feel like a million dollars.

We're going camping in France next summer, and I have to sort out all the plans with Mr . . . my dad.

I haven't called him that yet, but I think I might one day.

You should see Mum smile, too. I don't have to worry about her any more.

And that's the best bit of all. ■

Who's The Boss?

by Joan M. Newby

Tiger, my cat, got his own way in most things — and, remarkably, that included my choice of boyfriend!

ILOOKED at Gary as he nursed his scratched hand, and wavered between sympathy for him and annoyance at the way he had yelled at my cat. "You've frightened him away," I accused.

"He'll be back, like the proverbial bad penny." Gary held out his wounded hand for closer inspection. "Just look what he did to me."

"He was defending himself. He always sits on the settee and you'd no right to turf him off," I told him.

"I'm sick of being covered in cat hairs every time I sit down." He regarded his scratched hand mournfully. "He's drawn blood!"

"Oh, don't be such a baby!" I went for the disinfectant and dabbed the scratch with it before applying a dressing. I gave him a kiss which brought a beaming smile to his face.

"Cup of tea?" I asked. "Brandy? Smelling salts?"

He aimed a cushion at me and I escaped to the tiny kitchen and switched on the kettle. I heard a mewing at the front door, and opened it to let Tiger in. "You were put outside in disgrace," I lectured him as he stood gazing up at me. "If I were you, Tiger, I'd lie low for a while. It was very naughty of you to scratch poor Gary."

Tiger gave me a yellow-eyed stare and sauntered off into the bedroom, tail in the air like a banner.

"He's back, isn't he?" Gary said with a grimace, when I took the tea-tray into the lounge. "I can sense his evil presence."

"Don't exaggerate — he's only a cat. And he won't trouble you, he's having a nap on the bed." I handed Gary his tea. "Surely you're not scared of a little cat?"

"Of course not!" Gary glared at me. "I just don't like cats — they're such sneaky animals. I'm not surprised that people used to associate them with witches and black magic and that kind of thing."

"Oh, come on, there's nothing sinister about Tiger," I protested.

"Oh, no? Look at the way he sits and stares at us whenever I put my arm round you. He never even blinks. Talk about being chaperoned . . . he's always around!"

"I want you both to be friends," I said weakly.

"You think more of that old fleabag than you do of me." "That's childish jealousy, and you know it."

"Just because he was here first . . ." Gary continued as if I hadn't spoken.

"He was company for me before I met you," I reminded him, thinking back to my first days in the flat.

ISTILL found it painful, remembering the loneliness of those first weeks in a new job, in a strange town.

I had been lucky in finding such a nice flat, but at first the brilliant social life I had pictured showed no signs of materialising.

The girls I worked with in the office either had husbands or boyfriends who took up all their time.

I ended up spending long, lonely evenings with only a portable TV for company.

One blustery autumn night, as I was making my supper in the kitchen, I heard a faint mewing outside. Opening the door, I found a small stripey cat sheltering forlornly under a bush.

"You poor thing!" I exclaimed, bringing it indoors and drying it with a towel.

I warmed some milk which it wolfed down as if it had been starving for days. There was no collar or name-tag round its neck, and, although I reported my find at the police station, no-one claimed the little cat.

I decided he could stay, and called him Tiger.

It made all the difference to me, having Tiger strolling out to meet me when I came home each evening.

I had been in the flat nearly six months, and Tiger had grown large and sleek, when I met Gary Summerson in a vegetarian bar where I sometimes went for a snack lunch.

He was a partner in a shop that sold tapes and videos, not far, as it turned out, from the office where I worked. He started to pick me up from work in his car, and we would go out — to the cinema, or for a drink in a country pub. I felt really at ease with him, as if we'd known each other for ages.

The first time I invited him back to my flat, however, Gary almost took off when Tiger appeared.

"You didn't tell me you had a cat!" he exclaimed.

"Are you allergic to cats?" I asked, sensing problems.

"They don't give me asthma or anything like that, but I don't particularly like them."

"Why don't you like them?" I persisted.

"No special reason. Some people don't like spiders — I don't like cats. Maybe something happened when I was a kid — I don't know."

"I'm sure you'll take to Tiger once you get to know him," I said hopefully. "You will try, won't you?"

He flashed me a feeble imitation of his normally cheerful smile and replied, "I'll do my best, but don't expect miracles."

I watched as he skirted round Tiger to get to the settee where he sat down, keeping a wary eye on his enemy.

"I'll give him his supper," I said, and speedily lured Tiger into the kitchen.

Out of consideration for Gary's feelings, I shut Tiger in the kitchen while we had our meal. His outraged yowls, however, plus the sound of his sharp claws tearing at the door, forced me to let him out.

"He won't bother you," I told Gary, as he glanced at Tiger with alarm. "Just ignore him."

But Tiger must have decided he wanted to be loved. By way of making himself irresistible, he jumped up on Gary's knee and dug his claws in.

"Well brought-up cats do not treat guests like that," I scolded Tiger.

"He's taken a fancy to you," I told Gary, who was brushing cat hairs off his trousers.

"You could have fooled me," he growled.

DURING the weeks that followed, the antagonism between the two of them grew.

Whenever Gary came to the flat, Tiger made his presence felt. He seemed to take great delight in catching Gary unawares by launching himself on to his knee, or dropping down on to his shoulder, apparently from outer space.

Sometimes he would plant himself, just out of reach, and sit glaring at Gary.

But the crunch came about a week after the incident of the scratched hand.

Gary, carrying the tea-tray on his way from the kitchen, tripped over Tiger, who had been lurking in the shadows. The tray shot out of Gary's hands, tea spilled all over his trousers, and he twisted an ankle.

"I could have broken my neck! He did that on purpose!."

"It was an accident, Gary. Tiger's only a little cat."

"Scorpions aren't exactly giant-sized, but they can kill — size has nothing to do with it."

"He senses you're afraid of him and it makes him hostile," I said, and knew at once I had said the wrong thing.

"I'm not afraid of a cat!" He glowered at me. "I've told you before, I simply don't like them."

"You mentioned something could have happened when you were a child," I said tentatively. "Perhaps a cat jumped into your pram and it's left you with this phobia?"

Not surprisingly, this made matters worse. Gary's face turned crimson.

"Phobia? You're trying to make out that I'm dotty? You're the one with the hang-ups — you're besotted with that mangy creature! He comes first with you, every time!"

"If that's what you think, you'd better leave!" I yelled back, by now as hopping mad as he was. "Right then! You can have your flea-bitten soul-mate all to yourself, and I hope," he finished viciously, "that you'll both be very happy! Goodbye."

50

He strode out of the flat, banging the door behind him.

I was so angry, that for a while I didn't realise what had happened. Afterwards, however, I had to face the bleak fact that Gary had walked out on me.

I cried myself to sleep that night.

When I awoke next morning, I felt as if a huge black cloud was hanging over me. It took all my strength of mind to get up and go to the office.

It was an endless day and, when I got home, an endless night stretched ahead of me. Tiger came to welcome me, rubbing himself against my legs, but not even he could fill the gap left by Gary's departure.

I was due for a fortnight's leave and had meant to tell Gary about it and ask if he could arrange some time off from the shop, but we had quarrelled before I had a chance to mention it.

I hadn't been home for a while and, after some thought, I decided to spend my holiday with my family. Being back in familiar places among people who loved me might help to ease my aching heart, or so I hoped.

I checked with Mrs Prentiss, the lady who had the flat above mine, and who usually kept an eye on Tiger while I was away. She agreed to look after him for a fortnight.

MY fortnight at home passed slowly. I went for long walks with Dad and the two dogs, went shopping in the nearby market-town with Mum, and was teased and made the butt of practical jokes by my brothers, yet I felt a world away from the old life.

I phoned Mrs Prentiss twice to check on Tiger, but there was no answer.

At last it was time to leave. The return journey passed quickly, and I was soon back at my flat.

I let myself in, expecting Tiger to meet me. Instead, it was Gary who appeared.

"What are you doing here?" I gasped.

"Aren't you pleased to see me?" he asked nervously.

I swallowed hard, then flung all inhibitions to the wind and hurled myself at him. "Of course I'm pleased to see you!" I cried, and he held me as if he would never let me go. "I've been at my parents', but I missed you every minute!"

"I know where you've been. Mrs Prentiss told me. I came round the day after you'd left because I couldn't keep away any longer. She was here in the flat feeding Tiger and she was in a bit of a tizzy."

"Was she? Why?" I asked.

"Her eldest daughter had just had her second baby, earlier than expected, and Mrs P. felt she was needed to help take care of her grandson, only she didn't like to leave Tiger."

"Why didn't she ring me? I left the number in case of emergencies." I was still puzzled.

"She probably would have done, later, but she hated to spoil your holiday. Anyway, I took over and she went back to her own flat to pack."

I stared at him as what he had said registered. "You took over?"

"I promised to look after Tiger and the flat. That's what I've been doing for the last fortnight, and why I'm here now."

"But you can't stand cats — especially Tiger!" I reminded him.

He shuffled his feet nervously. "Well, he kind of grows on you," he muttered, embarrassed.

"While you were away, I went to the library and read up about phobias." He paused.

"I discovered that one way of dealing with a phobia is to get yourself used to being with whatever it is you're phobic about.

"I thought I'd try it out with Tiger, and with you and Mrs Prentiss away, I had the perfect opportunity."

"And has it worked?" I asked.

"I was determined to make it work." He gathered me even closer in his arms. "You and Tiger go together and I wasn't going to give you up for him, or any daft phobia!"

"Oh, Gary!" I was touched beyond belief.

Then I thought a little. "You could have rung me, the number was by the phone."

"And spoil the surprise?" He beamed down at me. "Besides, I knew you'd worry if you found out I was in charge of Tiger."

"I suppose I would." I sighed, and then, jolted by the thought, exclaimed, "Where is Tiger? I haven't seen him yet."

"I let him out for a stroll. He should be back by now."

Gary opened the door and Tiger marched in, carrying a dead mouse in his mouth.

He completely ignored me and stalked steadily up to Gary, obviously indignant because, in his view, I had deserted him for a whole fortnight.

On reaching Gary, he dropped the mouse on the floor and waited for some reaction.

"Well now," Gary said, bending down to inspect the poor little corpse. "That's decent of you, old fellow, giving me first chance."

As if satisfied, Tiger deliberately turned his back on me and marched off to the lounge, leaving Gary to scoop up his "trophy" and dispose of it.

"Don't worry," he said consolingly. "He'll soon come round and be friends with you again."

I smiled happily. After all, in this flat, Tiger was the boss! ■

Lucky Thirteen

by Carol Marsh

Her first teenage birthday didn't feel all that different. Then she realised it was up to her to make it special . . .

"SO I don't want a party this year, Dad," Gemma said. "I'll be thirteen, and I've been thinking, it's a bit — well — babyish, all that ice-cream and pass-the-parcel stuff!"

"Are you sure, love?" Her dad frowned down at her, his eyes wearing that faraway look he'd had so often these past few empty months. "I was going to phone Auntie Pam, and ask her to organise —"

"No!" Gemma said more forcefully than she'd intended, and her face filled with colour as she turned away.

This time last year, she thought in spite of herself, biting her lip to hold back the tears, Mum had the party cupboard filled with things, even though she knew she wasn't going to be here.

"Honestly, Dad," she finished, as she moved towards the stairs, "none of my friends are having parties this year. It's really old-fashioned!"

"Well, you know best, I s'pose, Gem." Dad sighed and shook his head.

A S he moved away, mumbling something about letting him know if there was something else she'd rather do, Gemma breathed a sigh of relief.

She wondered what he would say if he knew Sarah Marshall's parents were taking her out for a grown-up meal for her 13th. And Lucy Tranter was celebrating becoming a teenager by going, with her big brother, to her first rock concert.

"I'll be in the garage if you want me," Dad went on, picking up his coat a moment later. "There's a little job needs done to the car."

Since Mum died, there always seemed something — big or little — that needed done to the car.

As she watched him go down the front path, his shoulders bent, Gemma recalled how Auntie Pam, on her last visit, had exclaimed, "You really can't go on like this, you know, Andy — moping, and burying yourself away! It's the last thing Susan would've wanted, and apart from that, you've got Gemma to think about!"

He had been thinking about Gemma last night when, his face stiff with pain and embarrassment, he had first brought up the subject of the party.

"Gem — it's your birthday next week, isn't it? Time to start — well — planning things."

"Things?" Gemma's heart had squeezed inside her as, remembering now, it squeezed again. Carefully, she had avoided his deeply-troubled brown eyes.

"Your party, love!" For a second, he'd seemed almost animated, like the dad he used to be, and she'd caught at her breath.

Then the sadness came back, like an echo. "You know you've always had a party. Your — your mum —"

Mum wrote out invitations for all the kids in my class, one year. Again, the voice of memory claimed her attention, causing more pain. She clattered up the stairs and into her room. I was everybody's friend for ages . . .

She sighed as she sat down on the bed, and began to take her homework out of the schoolbag she'd discarded on the floor the night before.

She tried not to think of all the other years — all the other parties — but she couldn't help it.

There was her seventh birthday party — the one that almost got cancelled through chickenpox.

Mum made a cake covered in Smarties — "a spotty cake to match the spotty guests," she said. She'd turned what could have been a disaster into something special.

It was only Mum who had ever been able to do that, Gemma thought wistfully, her eyes straying from her books. Auntie Pam tried, helping out with the cooking and shopping, and letting Gemma go to her house straight from school when Dad had to work late.

But you couldn't expect her to be the same.

RESTLESSLY, Gemma rose from the bed and walked to the window. Down below, she could see the garage, with no sign of Dad.

She stared for a long time, wondering what he was doing, thinking again of how he had changed since Mum died.

At one time, she remembered, he used to laugh a lot, making jokes and pulling faces that had them all in stitches.

"We don't need a TV with you around, Andy Armstrong!" Mum used to say, her blue eyes shining with love.

But then, quite suddenly it seemed, Mum had to go into hospital for some routine tests.

"I'll be all right, Gemma — don't you worry!" Gemma closed her eyes, almost able to hear the soft, consoling voice, the night before the operation. "You just look after your dad — cheer him up. He's taking it hard, my not being very well."

For a while, when Mum came home that first time, they had all cheered one another up, Gemma remembered now.

"Now that nasty business is over, we can make a fresh start, Susie, darling!" her dad had said with relief, hugging the somehow frail figure of Mum close. "How about if we all go on a nice, long holiday, somewhere warm?"

But Mum had just smiled and shaken her head.

"No, Andy, I think I'd rather just recuperate here," she'd said. "Apart from that, I've got Gemma's birthday party to think about."

That year — was it really two years ago? — Gemma had been 11, and had new friends at the comprehensive school.

"Did your mum really make this cake?" Sarah Marshall had said enviously.

When Gemma nodded, looking proudly at the still delicate, but happy, figure handing out serviette-wrapped slices, Sarah had gone on, "I always have to have frozen gateau from the supermarket!"

"Nothing wrong with frozen gateau!" Gemma jumped, as she seemed to hear again Mum's voice, as she came and handed Sarah her parcel. "It takes all sorts of things to make a party."

Things like party-poppers and crazy balloons — hats and crackers. And lots of little tins and jars of goodies, carefully collected over the weeks before Mum went into hospital for the last time.

Gemma paced restlessly around the small room, her thoughts unwillingly returning to last year's celebration, when she was 12.

"You must have your party as usual!" Mum had insisted, her face so peaky but full of conviction as she reached for Gemma's hand. "Everything's there waiting, and you know the invitations have already gone out!"

"But you won't be there!" Gemma had sobbed, hiding her hot face in the cold sheets.

Her mum had smoothed back her daughter's long, fair hair.

"You must still have it!" she'd repeated firmly. "A party's special — and some are more special than others."

Next week's party — to celebrate her 13th birthday — would have been one of those, Gemma realised for the millionth, painful time. A teenager's party!

She closed her eyes, her heart thudding as she thought of how excited Mum would have been, organising it all — making sure it was really different.

But Mum was no longer here, and without her, her own and Dad's lives were grey and empty. Nothing seemed to matter any more, each day following the next, something to be got through, rather than enjoyed.

SUDDENLY unable to bear her thoughts any more, Gemma took her jacket from the back of the door.

She'd go and see for herself what Dad was doing in the garage — ask if he'd like to go for a walk in the park or maybe to the outskirts of the crowded, Saturday afternoon town.

As she slipped out of the house and down the path, she tried not to think of her birthday and the fact that her friends had started to look at her doubtfully.

"Don't suppose you'll be having a party this year, Gemma?" Lucy Tranter had said, and then, as somebody nudged her, had gone on quickly to talk about her own plans for the rock concert.

"Dad?" A few moments later, Gemma opened the garage door quietly and stepped inside, blinking in the strange, half light.

Dad didn't see her as she stepped towards the car. He was just sitting, not in the driving seat, but in the passenger seat — in Mum's seat.

He had the rug Mum used to wrap around her knees on a long journey over his shoulders, as if he were really cold.

He looked lost and sad, and so unbearably lonely that Gemma felt something snap inside her. She just stared, as if she couldn't believe her eyes.

Then, as if from nowhere, she seemed to hear Mum's voice again — like a nudge, desperate and inescapable. Look after your dad, Gemma. Cheer him up!

In that moment, she knew what she had to do, the only thing, if she and Dad were going to survive and somehow get over this terrible thing that had happened to them.

Setting her chin firmly, Gemma stepped right up to the parked car and opened the driver's door.

"I've changed my mind, Dad," she said quietly, as he looked at her in quick surprise. "I do want a party this year — but not a kid's one."

"What — what do you want then, Gem?" His alarm momentarily took the desolation out of his pale face.

Encouraged, Gemma got into the driving seat.

"I — I want guests, not friends," she planned, feeling his interest grow in spite of himself in the stunned silence. "No jelly or baby games — real music, and a new dress. Auntie Pam can come and help me choose if she likes.

"Oh — and as most of us will be teenagers, I suppose we'll have to have dancing and ask some boys."

"A — a buffet might be a good idea." She had run out of steam when Dad's almost shy suggestion came. "That way, we can buy a lot of the stuff already prepared."

"Brill!" A burst of something like happiness seemed to come from nowhere and light up the inside of the car.

Gemma leaned across and hugged her dad, blanket and all, feeling him gently ruffle her hair.

"Come on then, Dad," she said busily, a few moments later. "Let's go in and have a cup of tea and make some lists. We've got a lot to do before next week!"

This party, she realised, knowing her mum would have been proud of her, was going to be the most special of all. ■

The

SADIE PHILIPS had been single now for exactly a year. She drank a toast to those first, traumatic months when, first sadness, then relief had been her dominating emotions. Then she drank another toast — to the joy of living alone!

She could do exactly what she pleased, when and where! Her weekends were spent putting the Sadie imprint on the small, terraced two-up-and-two-down where their marriage had finally petered out, among piles of rubble, bricks, ballast and split bags of cement.

Adrian had begun so many projects which were never finished.

Independent Kind

She'd struggled hard to be her own woman. The last thing she needed was a new man in her life!

by Stella Whitelaw

The little house then became a haven of peace and quiet. She had loved Adrian — once — and that was the real grief of it.

He had bowled her over from their very first meeting — a tall, bearded draughtsman, amusing and attractively boyish.

And it had taken Sadie several years to discover that she did not actually want to be married to a boy. She wanted to be married to a man.

She obliterated all traces of Adrian, turning the second bedroom, which he had used as a darkroom/workshop for his photography, into a dressing-room.

Her sewing machine came out of cold storage and, after studying the latest fashions, she began to make herself some new clothes.

And she sold the hideous old table and chairs, which instantly enlarged the matchbox sitting-room.

Out with the table also went traditional, three-course cooking — meals were now taken in the kitchen, or on a tray on her knees.

Adrian had always expected enormous meals and his endless piles of washing had been gargantuan.

Sadie could also give more time to her work as personal assistant to the sales manager of a hosiery firm. Sadie had been doing a considerable amount of her boss's work for years.

But now every report, chart and sales analysis she produced for him had to be noticed, she decided.

She was going to be successful — she could feel it in her bones.

For the first time, she'd been invited to attend the firm's annual conference in Bournemouth.

"I'll enjoy that very much," she said to Oswald Harris, her boss, the south-eastern sales manager. "Thank you for including me, Mr Harris."

"You deserve a break," Oswald Harris had pointed out. Sadie gave a small, wary smile. She knew Mr Harris was retiring soon to Bexhill, to a flat overlooking the sea and the companionship of a brown spaniel called Dolly.

So, she was going to use every minute of that conference making sure she was fairly considered for Mr Harris's job!

SHE bought flowers on her way home to celebrate and did posies for every room, even the bathroom.

Adrian, she remembered now, had never noticed flowers.

On Saturday afternoon, feeling the need for another treat, she went along to an art gallery, watching the people as much as looking at the paintings.

"If you have a couple of hundred pounds to spare, the row of excellent seascapes on the right are mine," someone said in a modest voice. "I beg your pardon?" Sadie said questioningly, swinging round.

"I've been watching you," the man went on. "You were taking such a keen interest that I immediately thought, there's a prospective buyer. She can't make up her mind, though — all she needs is a little nudge."

"Wrong!" Sadie exclaimed. "I was thinking about some prints I have that need framing.

"They're stuck in the cupboard under the stairs and they reproach me every time I get out the vacuum.

"Framing's so expensive, though."

"Don't I know it! I usually go round the Sunday markets and, quite often, find suitable old frames.

"In fact, some of them are really beautiful . . . often better than my paintings."

"If your paintings are good enough to hang in this gallery, then they can't be that bad," Sadie pointed out. "Don't be so modest. Show them to me. Tell me all about them."

Sadie only said it to be polite, because he sounded so hesitant about his work, and his paintings did look interesting — pale fascinating seascapes with wonderfully-delicate touches of colour.

60

She peered closer to read the signature. Ed Ryan — it seemed a very unassuming name for an artist.

"I can't buy one," she said. "I'm skint. I've a whole mortgage to take care of."

"A whole mortgage?" he repeated sagely. "Obviously a woman of property."

"It's as tiny as a doll's house," she said. "But it's all my own and, even if I say so myself, very pleasant."

"I don't think I could live in a house." He grinned. "Not any more. Not a proper house — it'd be too much like a prison."

"Where do you live then?" she asked curiously. His jeans and shirt were neat and clean, so he obviously wasn't sleeping rough.

"I've a Land-Rover, a dog and a caravan. I go where I like, along the coast mostly. I'm a nomad, a gipsy, a wanderer."

"Ah . . ." was about as much as Sadie could say. She was out of her depth with gipsies and nomads. "I'm going to Bournemouth soon."

His eloquent eyes smiled suddenly. "You'll like Bournemouth," he predicted. "It has a beautiful sea and spectacular cliffs."

THEY had a cup of coffee afterwards, companionably, talking a lot, and then Ed Ryan disappeared as suddenly as he had appeared.

He hadn't said much about himself, only that he had once been an accountant and could fill in a tax form.

Sadie enjoyed his company, but was glad he had not suggested seeing her again.

How could he, anyway? A dog, a Land-Rover and a caravan were not the hallmarks of a conventional living. And all thoughts of him went out of her mind when she opened Monday's post. Among the bills was a letter from a firm of solicitors — her godmother had died and left her a house in the North!

Sadie was stunned by the news. She had hardly known her godmother and felt very unworthy of the bequest. It's rather old and ramshackle, and in need of modernisation, the solicitor had pointed out in his letter.

At work, she blurted out the news to Mr Harris. "Oh, so you'll be giving up your job and moving, will you?" he said. "I'll cancel your hotel booking for the conference."

"No, you won't!" Sadie declared firmly. "I'm not going to give up my job and I'd still like to go to the conference."

SOME days later, when her ex-husband appeared on her doorstep, she automatically asked him in. She regretted it the instant Adrian set foot in her home.

"Who's a lucky girl?" He laughed, giving her a big hug. "Another house!"

"How did you know?"

61

He tapped his nose, then, mysteriously. "I have my sources. Old boys' network, you know." He threw himself down in his old armchair, feet stretched out on the rug.

"Ah, home." He sighed, eyeing the room. "I've really missed all this. Hey, where's the dining-table? And the showcase for my trophies?"

"Trophies, you say?"

"Never mind. We can soon . . ." He stopped, but Sadie could read his mind — his thoughts were almost lit up in neon — soon put it up again, was what he'd been going to say.

Not on your nelly, Sadie thought. But she merely added, "Would you like some coffee?" wishing she wasn't always so darned polite.

"Smashing." He launched into a recital of what he had been doing. He had been moving around a lot. He had not bought a new place or settled anywhere.

He had eventually gone home to roost, where his mother prepared his huge meals and washed and tidied up after him.

He put his coffee cup on the floor, got up and began roaming round the house, making comments on all the changes.

"Hey, what's this?" he called down, blinking at the mirrored doors of his former darkroom.

"My dressing-room!"

"Dressing-room!" he chortled. "Still, you'll be able to move out now and get somewhere bigger."

"I don't want somewhere bigger," Sadie pointed out. "I couldn't cope with somewhere bigger. This house is just the right size for me."

"But it's practically a cupboard!" he exclaimed. "You'll be able to afford exactly what you want now.

"I've always fancied one of those ranch-type houses, sprawling and low slung, with lots of wood.

"Did I tell you I've taken up carpentry?"

Sadie heard the alarm bells ringing madly.

When he asked if he could stay the night as his mother had gone to visit her sister, she offered him the sofa.

A WEEK later Adrian was still there, making plans and suggestions, sprawled on the sofa.

Sadie felt her independence crumbling. She knew she was a fool, but she was sorry for him. "I'm going to Bournemouth next weekend to the firm's annual conference," she told him. "You can stay in the house while I'm away, but then I think you ought to look seriously for a place of your own."

"Darling, is that really necessary?" he said, taking her in his arms. "Can't we start again, please, darling?" he went on. "We're getting on so well, now. Things will be different. We could have a big house, every labour-saving gadget — dishwasher, waste-disposal unit, you name it."

He was very persuasive and handsome — and she had once loved him.

62

"We could be so happy," he said, sweeping her round the room, knocking over some flowers.

"We'll have a second honeymoon, somewhere exotic. I'll make you happy, Sadie, I promise."

Sadie extracted herself from his arms and went down on her knees to retrieve the flowers — he didn't move to help her.

"I'll tell you when I get back from Bournemouth," she said, picking up the tiny, fragile petals from the carpet.

She felt like those crushed petals — Adrian was treading all over her again.

B OURNEMOUTH was refreshing. The stiff sea breeze blew away some of the cobwebs of indecision and the stifling influence of her ex.

The conference wasn't exactly the den of intrigue that Mr Harris had always implied. The meetings were informal but constructive and Sadie quickly discovered that, by asking the right, pertinent questions, she showed she knew more than just how to feed paper into a printer.

Late one afternoon at the end of a busy session, Sadie put on jeans and a jersey and went for a stroll along the beach.

There hadn't been time before. Yes, the sea was beautiful and the cliffs white and majestic — they had a timeless quality.

Perhaps that was why Ed Ryan always painted the sea.

She walked a long way. She passed the famous chines, passed the houses, hotels and beach huts.

She wanted to walk for ever — it seemed an admirable plan. No more worrying or wondering — no more Adrian.

"You can't get any farther unless you've got climbing boots," the voice of Ed Ryan said suddenly from a perch some way up. He was working — a sketchbook lay on the ledge, alongside a box of charcoal and pastels.

"I hoped I might see you."

Sadie smiled. She was pleased to see him, too. "How did you know I'd be here?"

"You told me," he said, frowning slightly. "Remember? Over coffee. You told me about coming to Bournemouth this weekend .

"But I was beginning to give up any hope of seeing you. Look, I don't suppose you'd care to share a caravan supper with me tonight? Sausages under the stars? Very romantic."

Sadie laughed, absurdly pleased to be asked.

"Oh, Ed, I can't. Tonight is the big, formal, sit-down dinner. I daren't miss it.

"I'll be meeting everybody, mixing with all the directors. It's when I'll be able to find out if they're really considering me for Mr Harris' job."

"Then you must go," he said. "That's important!"

"It's more than important," she said. "It's crucial."

And she told him about her godmother's house and Adrian moving back in again.

Ed listened intently, sometimes putting in a question to clarify a point. But all the time, his slender hands were working with the charcoal, on his sketch of the gathering clouds.

At one point, he took off his glasses, wiping the lenses with a paint rag. His eyes were the warmest brown she had ever seen, kind and a little unfocused.

She supposed he couldn't see her properly, so she didn't feel embarrassed about scrutinising his face.

He wasn't handsome, not classically good looking, but oh, there was a gritty, something special, there!

Sadie shook herself mentally — she was not going to get trapped again.

"It's going to rain," he said suddenly, packing up his things. "I'll see you back to your hotel. Put on your glad rags and go in there fighting, lady."

He took her hand to help her down from the rocks, but didn't let go.

He left her casually at the hotel steps. "See you next year, babe. Sock it to them!"

She felt a pang when he walked away. Next year seemed an incredibly long time away.

But then she got caught up in getting ready for the dinner . . .

B efore she left to return on the early Monday train to London, she received a typewritten note from the managing director.

Would she kindly present herself at his office on Tuesday morning at ten o'clock? Relief washed over her as she sat on the train, watching the countryside speed by.

Bournemouth had been unreal in a way — she might almost have imagined it all.

But the note was tangible enough and she was going back to the reality of Adrian camped out in her house.

She had to deal with him — and she could give away her godmother's house, if she wanted, to some charitable cause— perhaps the homeless, orphans, or the disabled could put it to good use.

Once Adrian discovered that her capital had gone, he would go, too. She was not hurt. She just understood him.

A S she turned the corner that evening, laden with her weekend case, she could hardly believe what she saw outside her house.

Parked by her tiny, terraced front door was a muddy Land-Rover and a caravan, taking up a lot of space. A brown-faced dog peered at her from the back of the vehicle.

She got out her key, aghast, wondering what might confront her.

Adrian flung open the door, screwdriver in hand, bits of sawdust in his hair.

64

"At last," he declaimed. "Just who is this person who has come to frame your prints?"

Sadie could see Ed on his knees, cleaning a heavy, old carved frame. He looked up, his dark face expressionless.

"He's the person who has come to frame my prints," she said.

"He seems to know his way around the house," Adrian went on, tripping over his toolbox — he had been putting up shelves for his photo albums.

"You hardly need a route map for a house of this size," Sadie declared wryly.

She put the kettle on, but Ed was already getting out the milk and the mugs. She daren't look at him — the "totally-at-home" act was move perfect.

"Oh, sorry," she said to Ed, looking into the biscuit tin. "Your favourite gingernuts have all gone."

"Look, Sadie," Adrian said, filling the doorway. "I want to know exactly whats' going on."

"I don't think it's any of your business," Sadie pointed out reasonably. "We're divorced, remember?

"And I think it's time you and your hobbies found somewhere else to mess up. This is my home now and I don't want anything in it to remind me of you."

Ed wandered into the sitting-room, picking up tools and bits of wood as he went.

He put all the debris into Adrian's arms and steered him towards the door.

"If I find anything else of yours, I'll send it on," he said firmly. "Just forward an address."

Adrian's mouth fell open. He hardly knew what was happening. Then he found himself on the doorstep, the door slammed firmly in his face.

Sadie looked at Ed, not really knowing what to say.

"That was a short year," she finally remarked ridiculously.

"Did you get the promotion?" he asked.

"I think so. I'm going to see the managing director tomorrow."

He nodded, drinking his tea.

"Good," he said. "I'll be off then. I'm driving down to Cornwall tonight."

Her heart sank. She didn't want him to go and, yet, the only way to keep this strange, sincere and wonderful man was to let him go.

Swiftly, he cleared up his odds and ends . . . tidiness that came from living in a caravan.

She stood on the step to see him drive off.

The dog gave him an ecstatic welcome as he climbed aboard.

Ed put the Land-Rover in gear, but didn't move off.

"Sausages under the stars, sometime?" he shouted. "The invitation still stands."

Sadie's face broke into a wide smile.

"I accept!" She laughed, waving, knowing that, one day,
he would be back. ■

KING OF THE CASTLE

Five year old Mark named him.
Seven year old Sue tamed him.
Nothing like children on a farm
To turn your life style upside down.
Caruso is the children's cock.
His voice is raised at dawn.
They love his brilliant feathers
And insist that he's kept warm.
When winter nights are cold and dark
Caruso finds the house an ark.
Cross the yard and bang on the door
Not for him the henhouse floor.
The children laugh as he flies to the chair
And perches himself to stay cosy there.
Outside in the yard his harem can stay.
None dare share Caruso's day.
Folk buying eggs go off and talk
Of the indoor bird that is Cock of the Walk.
There are often times when his screech at dawn
Makes me wish he had never been born.
But they laugh in the pub when I tell the saga
Of the cock that lives in front of our Aga.

A poem by Joyce Stranger,
inspired by an illustration by Mark Viney.

Kiss Today Goodbye

by Marian Hipwell

*In just twenty-four hours I had learned
the heart-breaking difference between
friendship and love . . .*

IT was the same restaurant they had gone to on their first date. Ever since
he had seen Angela hurrying to work this morning, Bill had known they
would end up here.

This morning he had been sheltering from the rain in a shop doorway
when he'd seen Angela hurry past with a companion on her way to work.

Despite the way she had been smiling up at her friend, she had looked
strained and confused.

And ever since then, Bill had known what he had to do. That was why he
had invited Angela to this restaurant again.

"I always did like this place." Angela glanced around briefly after the waiter had taken their order.

She was making an effort at brightness now, eyeing him tentatively when she thought he wasn't watching her.

"Yes, it's a special place in many ways," Bill murmured.

He saw the quick wariness in her eyes and felt saddened. There had never been wariness before between them.

How long was it now; a year almost? It seemed like only yesterday . . .

They had both been new in town, lonely, bewildered and desperately trying to find a foothold somewhere.

Finding each other out of all that had been something of a miracle. They had provided a haven for each other against the worst elements of being a stranger in a bustling, anonymous city.

Angela was watching him intently now, wondering, he guessed, just why he had rung with such urgency and told her he was taking her to dinner at The Miramare and would listen to no excuses.

"You look tired." He eyed her appraisingly. Yet it was the watchfulness which lurked within their blue depths as much as the circles under her eyes, which disturbed him.

Angela had never had time for secrets or constraint, until recently. Maybe he was imagining it, looking for excuses for what he was about to do?

No, never that, he decided.

She was talking quickly now, telling him how busy things were at work, how she wished she hadn't taken on two evening classes this term; telling him anything but what he really wanted to know.

He realised that she was talking to keep him from doing so, putting off what she knew he was going to say.

She continued to chatter on about anything and everything, illustrating her remarks with quick, nervous gestures and smiles which never reached her eyes.

"Angela —" He broke in at last, and something in his tone made her stop in mid-sentence. Now he had her attention, he didn't know quite what to say.

"— I think it's time we talked," he finished, wincing at the cliché.

Bill saw the alarm flash into her eyes, then vanish under a careful, arranged smile.

"You've been promoted, haven't you?" she asked. "That's why we're here celebrating, isn't it?"

She was begging him to confirm it, he realised. Begging him to agree that their being at this particular place at this particular time had nothing to do with their personal lives.

For a moment he was tempted to go along. Then, recalling her hurrying figure earlier in the day, head bent against the rain, he knew he couldn't.

THERE was a moment's respite while the waiter served their meal, smiling and making enthusiastic comments about the food. When he left, Bill had no further reason for delay.

"Actually, it's about us I wanted to talk." He reached out for her hand.

It's all right, he wanted to tell her. At least, it will be . . .

He looked down at her hand in his. In the subdued lighting of the restaurant, the jewelled ring on her finger couldn't be seen to best advantage.

He had bought it for her at Christmas and she had worn it ever since.

It glowed now with its own particular message, the inscription inside it which had caught both their imaginations.

Friendship endures.

And that's what it was, they had been quick to assure each other, as the assistant wrapped it up for them. A friendship ring. Nothing more, nothing less . . .

"I don't know how to start," he said helplessly after a moment.

"Then why bother?" she smiled. "Let's just eat this wonderful food and enjoy the evening."

It would be so easy to follow her lead, allow things to drift on. As they would have, he realised, if seeing her this morning hadn't jolted him into an awareness that something had to be done.

And Angela, tender-hearted Angela who wouldn't willingly hurt anyone, would never be the one to do it.

Bill took a deep breath, keeping her hand in his.

"I think it's time we let each other go," he said at last. He felt the sudden tenseness of her body, and tightened his hold on her fingers.

The moment was as difficult for her as it was for him. And when he looked into her eyes there was a mixture of surprise, relief she wasn't quick enough to hide . . . and pain.

For a moment they both sat watching the steam spiralling upward from the food they had so far both ignored.

At last, Bill made a restless movement. "Eat your food," he murmured.

They both needed some time to think.

Was he right to trust his instincts that it was time for a parting of the ways? There was affection and companionship between them, so was he chasing a dream, feeling that somehow there should be more?

Was it foolish to think that somewhere, if only they had the courage to reach out for it, there was this wild, surging feeling which neither of them could fail to recognise as anything other than love?

Or was he just over-romantic, looking for feelings which were only found in books?

Angela pushed her plate away, giving up all pretence of eating.

"Bill —" she was eyeing him tentatively, almost entreatingly.

"No, let me say my piece first." He spoke determinedly now, anxious to get it over with.

"I've had this feeling for a while that — well, that we're just going on together because we feel we ought to."

He sighed and ran a hand through his hair. "I'm not putting this right. I'm minimising everything we had — and still have.

"You're one of the best things that ever happened to me, Angela, and I'll never forget —"

"It's all right, Bill." She spoke quickly. "I know what you're trying to say. And I agree."

They were still holding hands, clinging almost desperately to the link which had bound them together through that first long winter and the summer months that followed.

Angela laughed shakily. "I thought, when you suggested coming here, that you were going to ask me to marry you or something."

Thank goodness I didn't, Bill thought. Thank goodness I spared us both that.

"I take it you would have turned me down?" He tried to speak lightly.

There was a glint of tears in Angela's eyes.

"Don't," he said gruffly.

"I can't help it . . ."

She took her hand from his and groped inside her bag for a tissue. Bill watched as she dabbed at her eyes. He was going to hate being without her.

Even now, she was still within his reach; all he had to do was murmur something about their waiting a while for their feelings to grow stronger, and they would be each other's prisoner again.

He swallowed. Could he just let her walk out of his life as he had told himself he could? Not if it meant letting her think that the long months of closeness between them had counted for nothing.

"I just feel there's more —" he said, desperate to explain and falling back on the trite phrases he had used to convince himself "— that this feeling we have for each other isn't — well, isn't the one for marriage."

Yet how did he know, until and unless he himself experienced that elusive feeling he sensed lay in wait for both of them?

How could he be sure he wasn't just throwing away the most precious thing his life would ever hold?

Yet he had to do it; ever since he'd seen the look on her face this morning he had known that.

"We were both lonely and missing home," Angela murmured unexpectedly. "Finding each other then was a lifeline for both of us."

So he wasn't the only one who'd sensed things were wrong, Bill thought.

"But we're on our feet now; we shouldn't be leaning on each other so much," she went on.

Is that what they had been doing, Bill wondered, leaning on each other? Or was she offering him a way out, now he'd brought things into the open — as anxious to end it as he apparently was?

"It wasn't just that," he said. "I'd hate you to think —"

"I know," Angela interrupted softly. "I know."

THEY had walked home slowly, hand in hand, just like always. It was one of those mild, smoky autumnal evenings and the wind chased damp leaves around their feet.

Was this what had brought it on, Bill wondered. Was autumn encouraging him to discard anything that was old and useless as if it were a dead leaf?

His fingers tightened convulsively on Angela's. No, never useless. Turning, he looked at her.

She was composed now. Obviously miserable, yet there was a relief there, too, he sensed, which told him he had been right to end it.

Reaching her door they paused, eyeing each other uncertainly.

"Well." Bill cleared his throat. "Here we are."

Here we are is right, he thought. At the parting of the ways and, so far as I'm concerned, with nothing in view but the prospect of lonely winter months ahead.

He shivered, suddenly feeling cold after the warmth of the restaurant. He felt her lips brush his cheek fleetingly.

"I do love you, you know." It was a mere whisper.

"And I love you," he whispered back.

What a pity it was that it hadn't been the right kind of love . . .

Angela turned and hurried towards her door, not wanting to prolong the parting. She was almost inside when she turned and looked back at him, still standing watching her.

"What about — about this?" She was indicating the ring on her finger. "Do you want it back?"

"No, it's yours." Bill spoke quickly. "I mean, after all, it was for friendship." He eyed her hesitantly. "We can still be friends, can't we?"

It was the time-honoured thing to say in situations like this, but he meant it. Not that he expected her to agree . . .

Angela looked down at the ring, then at him. She smiled but he saw the sadness in her eyes.

She wouldn't wear it again, he told himself as he turned and walked away. Did she understand why he had done it? Or had he hurt her so much she would never think of him again without bitterness?

IT was a few weeks before he saw her again. Weeks of working frantically to stop himself thinking, of overloud television programmes in the evening to blot out the silence in the flat.

This time he didn't slip into the nearest shop doorway.

The same man was with her. He had met him briefly, Bill recalled. He was the fair-haired newcomer to Angela's office who lived in the same block of flats and with whom she had got into the habit of walking to work.

The weather was bad, as it had been the first time, and Angela's shoulders were once more hunched against the rain. And she was still smiling up at her companion, the way she had been that other time.

But this time, Bill reflected, there was openness in it, not the strain he had witnessed before.

There was an air about her, too, as she laughed at something he had said, that told Bill she was on the way to finding that magical feeling he had sensed waited for them both somewhere.

Bill stole a glance at her companion. He looked a nice sort, Bill thought without rancour.

Then suddenly Angela saw him; the smile vanished and she looked uncertain.

Taking his hand from his pocket, Bill waved. And, as she raised a hand in acknowledgement, he caught the glint of the ring on her finger.

It flashed its message to him in a way no words of hers could ever have done.

Friendship endures, even after love has gone . . .

They continued on their separate ways then, his own heart lighter than it had been for weeks.

It was round the corner somewhere, waiting for him; that happiness he had seen on Angela's face moments ago.

It was a strange, yet exciting, feeling to know that somewhere walking through his future life towards him, was a girl who would look at him and love him.

He wished her Godspeed, this unknown girl who would justify the hardest decision he had ever taken.

And, from the bottom of his heart, he sent a wish for the best of everything to the girl in his past.

And a wish that they remain, forever, the best of friends . . . ■

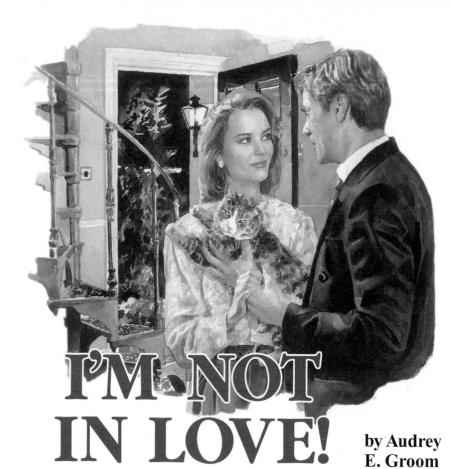

I'M NOT IN LOVE!

by Audrey E. Groom

The funny thing was, the more he said that, the less he believed it . . .

AT home in his little bed-sit, Gareth's ears were still ringing with Julie's sobs and recriminations, as he piled baked beans on to a slice of over-cooked toast.

Gloomily he carried the less than gourmet meal to his armchair, and sinking on to the well-worn seat, stared at the blank TV screen.

He didn't feel like switching it on. He didn't want to watch one more soap or one more romantic film. To be honest, he was right off romance — and the trouble it caused.

Take Julie now — she was a nice girl; attractive, fun to be with. They'd had some good times together. But he'd never said he loved her. And so why should she get so upset when he turned down the chance to visit her parents for the weekend?

He'd tried to explain that meeting parents was saying they were serious about each other.

"But I thought you loved me, Gareth," she'd stormed.

"I like you a lot, Julie, but —"

"I know your sort — always breaking girls' hearts," she interrupted.

He didn't go on with what he'd been about to explain.

What was the point in saying, "I never said I loved you, Julie," when Julie obviously had had the impression that he did?

It was the same with the women in his office.

Remarks floated around that gave him the impression they considered him some latter-day Casanova — loving and leaving girls in droves.

In fact he had only ever dated about half a dozen girls in his life. And he'd never yet been in love.

But he couldn't help that, could he? At least he'd never pretended something that he didn't feel. But it seemed you couldn't win with girls.

Gareth took his plate to the sink. So that was it then, he thought. At the tender age of 22, he'd finished with women.

THEN there was a knock at his door. And when Gareth opened it — there stood a girl!

Gareth was six feet two. This girl was shorter, with a round, smooth, dimpled face, beautiful eyes and a mass of auburn, wavy hair. In her arm she held a cat. Gareth swallowed hard.

After his thoughts of the last hour, he didn't quite understand why a sudden strange, warm, pleasant feeling was coursing through him.

He pulled himself up to his full height, took a deep breath and decided it was because of the cat she was holding. He was very fond of cats. "I'm sorry to bother you," the girl whispered, "but can I talk to you?"

Since he was going to have nothing more to do with girls, he didn't see why not. He held the door wide and smiled broadly. She smiled, too, and that strange warm feeling ran through Gareth again. "This little cat keeps scratching at my door," the girl confided. "I know we're not supposed to keep pets, but she's so sweet, I had to let her in . . .

"By the way, I moved into the room at the end of the corridor last week. I'm Sally."

"Oh! Did you?" Gareth said vaguely. For some reason he felt as if he were floating on a pink cloud.

"You're not listening, are you?" the girl said accusingly. Gareth took another deep breath.

"Oh! I am, I am," he said, giving her his full attention. "Look, tell me — about the cat."

The smile dimpled her face again.

"Well, I have to go out for a while, you see, and I don't like leaving her in my room — alone. So I was wondering . . . would you have her for me, just for an hour or two?"

"Sure. No problem."

Gareth put out his arms to take the cat and the girl gently lowered her into them. Their hands touched, sending shock waves through Gareth.

"Thank you ever so much. By the way, what's your name?"

"I'm Gareth."

"Right. I'll be back about ten, Gareth."

And as quickly as she had come, she was gone.

Gareth looked down at the cat.

Stroking the soft, furry, purring creature, he tried not to think about the girl who'd brought her.

After all, since he'd just decided to have nothing more to do with girls, there was no point in dwelling on the undeniable attractions of Sally. No point at all.

He wouldn't dream of asking her out, for instance. Definitely not.

LIKE to come out for a drink one evening?" he suggested when he handed back the cat.

"Well, if I can find another cat-sitter," she told him, "I'd like to. I could try asking old Mrs Barker upstairs."

"How about Friday, then?"

"Friday'll be fine, if Mrs B obliges."

"Great," he said with a grin.

Then as he closed the door, he thought, I've done it again. I'm supposed to have given up girls for good!

But he couldn't feel unhappy about it, either. Despite Julie's cool glances the next day, he knew he was still looking forward enormously to meeting Sally on Friday evening.

And he wasn't disappointed. Mrs Barker had agreed to look after the cat.

Sally was good company, fun to be with. But there was something much, much more than either of those. Something he couldn't define at first.

Just one thing bothered him now. He'd always been most careful not to give other girls the wrong impression by acting over-romantic, but he found himself longing to let Sally know how he felt . . .

In fact, it all happened quite naturally. One evening they were just about to cross a busy road. He thought a car was coming too fast for safety and impulsively grabbed Sally's hand to pull her back.

Only she didn't take hers away when the danger was past, but just kept it there in his; small, soft, and warm.

Gareth was delighted, and he was still holding Sally's hand when they reached her door.

"'Night, Sally," he said softly, looking down on the top of her glossy hair.

And he couldn't help himself, he bent down and planted a light kiss on her head.

She laughed and looked up, her pretty, dimpled face and shining eyes turned up to him in the moonlight.

Her soft, warm lips were inviting . . . And so he kissed them, too. And then he kissed them again. And again. And the whole world seemed to somersault.

"Goodnight, Gareth," she whispered, as she slipped into her room. And Gareth was left staring at the closed door and thinking that life would never be the same.

He was floating on that pink cloud again. And a feeling of intense happiness overwhelmed him.

AT least, it did until he was climbing into bed. Then it suddenly evaporated. And in its place he experienced the most awful nagging anxiety.

It had been a wonderful evening for him. He had been over the moon at walking home hand-in-hand with Sally and kissing her. But how did she feel about him?

True, she'd seemed to respond to his kisses. Or was that just his imagination — or extremely wishful thinking on his part?

Sleep eluded him. Suppose she didn't feel the same way about him? Suppose . . . and the awfulness of this thought enveloped him, suppose she only saw him as a friend, someone to have a pleasant evening with — just as he had seen Julie . . .

The thought set him on edge.

Some people might call it poetic justice, he presumed; he called it torture, self-inflicted torture.

Early next morning, he knocked at her door, but she'd already left for work. He spent a miserable day.

However, in the evening she was at his door as soon as he got home — with the cat in her arms again. His heart began to thud uncontrollably. She smiled up at him, making him go weak at the knees.

"Mrs Barker's out this evening, and I have to go out too, Gareth. Would you mind looking after her again, please."

It was a very matter-of-fact request. She seemed different from last night. Those mind-blowing few moments . . . But perhaps they hadn't been mind-blowing for her.

After all, where was she going tonight? To meet another guy? Someone she was really in love with?

Gareth took the cat from her and then spent a painful evening of jealousy and doubt.

He was even too miserable to make beans on toast for himself.

Instead, he sat nursing the cat and dreaming of what might have been, until Sally came home.

S HE looked so sweet and desirable, looking up at him when he answered the door. Don't run away, his heart pleaded.

"Coffee?" he asked her.

His heart leapt when she nodded and came inside.

Then she went over and began to stroke the cat where it lay on his chair.

"Well, did you have a nice evening?" he managed to ask her at last.

She shrugged.

"Well — no — not really."

In his rush to fill the cups, Gareth spilled water all over the place and clattered the cups in their saucers.

At last he carried the coffee to where she was sitting with the cat on her lap. He sat down opposite her. He stretched out a hand and gently touched her wrist.

"What went wrong, Sally?"

She smiled a faraway smile and a few moments passed. Then at last she spoke. "I've been going out with someone for a while, you see . . . but I thought perhaps it would be best if we didn't meet again. You see, I know now I'm not in love with him."

"You do?"

"Yes. Hasn't it ever happened to you like that, Gareth? That you've been out with someone and found, and found —"

"Yes, it has," Gareth said quickly, "it certainly has."

"And when you do fall in love —" Sally's voice faltered, but Gareth went on.

"When you do fall in love, you know that it's so different, and that it was worth waiting for, don't you?"

Suddenly he was off his chair and kneeling in front of her. His arms were around her and hers around him and the poor cat was somewhere in the middle.

They both laughed and leaned back and the cat stretched and jumped to the floor. Then they could embrace and kiss properly.

"I love you, Sally," Gareth whispered.

"I love you, too, Gareth."

Later, much later, when she'd gone and he was feeling happy and too restless to sleep, he actually switched on the TV. He didn't mind a nice romantic late-night film now.

Ws it only a few short weeks back that he had been sneering at romance and vowing that he'd finished with girls?

Well, of course he had, in fact he was finished with them now. All except one. His one and only. There'd only be Sally from now on.

And a cat, of course. They'd definitely have a cat when they were married. ∎

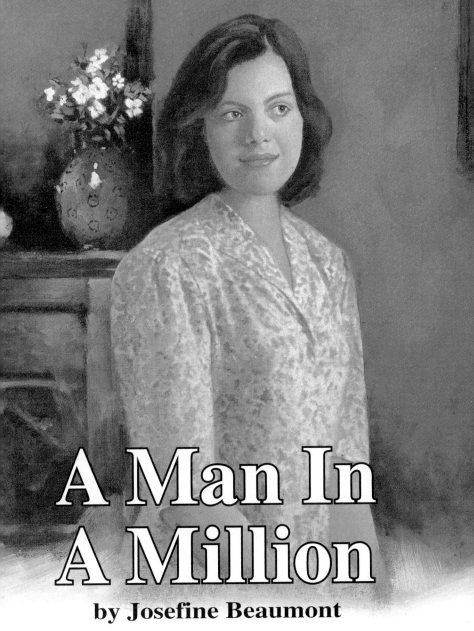

A Man In A Million

by Josefine Beaumont

I'd always been shy, a real shrinking violet. Yet from the moment I met him, I blossomed . . .

SOMETIMES, in the middle of a perfectly ordinary day, I stop and remember the woman I used to be, in that other life, when I was a different person.

I remember and I smile ruefully . . .

The truth was I should have left home years earlier. Imagine, a 37-year-old woman still living at home with her mother when she didn't have to!

But I never quite managed to summon the courage to take such a drastic step.

I told myself Mother wouldn't like it, but it was just an excuse. The truth was, I was afraid to find a flat. If I did, I'd be truly alone and that didn't bear thinking about.

So, I never left home, just like I never tried dieting. That was something else I should have done years ago! But I was cursed with an extremely healthy appetite.

I couldn't resist Mother's calorie-laden steak-and-kidney pies, her suet dumplings and fruit cakes, any more than I could deny myself her freshly-baked bread.

Mother was a superb cook and, I'm afraid, it all went into my mouth and on to my body with a vengeance. Like Topsy, I simply grew and grew.

It did nothing, of course, to assist me in the marriage stakes.

My younger sister, Jenny, on the other hand, could and did eat enough to sink a battleship and yet still stayed enviably thin.

It had to be glandular in my case, I'd tell myself glumly.

Jenny married a nice man called David Brooke. She was barely 20 then, and before she was 30 she had produced two fine sons and a daughter. I was jealous, I admit it.

In comparison, my life seemed dull and hopeless. I particularly envied Jenny her children.

Then fate, Cupid and Jenny stepped in and helped.

NORMALLY I hated parties and always tried to hide myself away in a corner, feeling like a great big blob.

Parties were always the same for me. Hardly anyone talked to me and I was never asked to dance . . . not that I wanted to dance.

I knew what I looked like dancing — like a demented jelly. Still, it would have been nice to be asked.

Anyway, Jenny's 10th wedding anniversary was one social event even I couldn't wriggle out of.

Worse still, Jenny insisted we went shopping together for a party dress. That was something else I hated, because I could never find a decent dress to wear.

It was over a silly dress in one of the big department stores that Jenny and I eventually ended up arguing.

Lifting a dress from one of the racks she exclaimed, "Isn't this gorgeous?

It would suit you perfectly, Judith!"

I stared at it, fuming inwardly with her. It was a sheaf of brilliantly-coloured blue silk and, to tell the truth, I doubt if I could have squeezed my thighs into it, let alone the rest of my body!

"I'd look like a barrage balloon in that!" I retorted tartly.

She flushed, but insisted, "You wouldn't, Judith. Trust me!"

I inspected the label — the price was enough to make the strongest heart fail.

"It's only a size sixteen!" I icily pointed out.

"You could diet," she suggested flatly. "There're two whole weeks before the party. Time enough."

"Do you think I've never tried dieting?" I asked.

"No, Judith." She looked straight into my eyes. "I don't think you ever have."

"You should try minding your own business, Jenny!" I declared icily.

"And you, Judith, should try dieting seriously for once!"

"I'm going home."

"So, go!" She threw up her hands. "Run away. Just like you always do. Hide behind your weight . . . because that's what you're doing.

"That's what you've always done. Hidden from life! Well, if you want to spend the rest of your days hanging on to Mama's skirts, then go ahead!"

"I'll wait for you in the car," I said coldly and marched out of the shop, trying desperately not to cry.

When she finally arrived, we drove home in silence.

"Are you coming in for coffee?" she asked meekly, and I shook my head. She sighed and thrust a bag at me, saying timidly, "I bought the dress for you, Judith."

"You bought me a dress two sizes too small?" I demanded angrily. "Fine, Jenny, wonderful!" I went on. "I can go to your party looking like an over-stuffed sausage, is that it?"

"No," she said quietly. "I wanted to give you something beautiful, Judith. Because you're my sister and I love you and because we've never argued before and I can't stand it."

My anger deflated like a punctured tyre. "Do you think being thin's going to change my life?" I sighed.

"I'm thirty-seven years old, Jen. Let's face it. Fat or thin, life has passed me by. What's the point in me even trying?"

"The point is," she said softly, "you're a beautiful woman, warm and loving and it angers me to see it all going to waste."

"OK, I'll try — for you," I whispered.

But she shook her head and said firmly, "Oh, no, Judith, not for me. Do it for yourself!"

And I did!

DO you want the truth? It was torture, pure and simple. Every single morning, I faithfully swallowed a glass of warm water, ate half a grapefruit and a square of toast so small it hardly hit my tongue before it disappeared into my empty stomach.

I lunched on cottage cheese and celery and, for dinner, I had clear soups or yoghurt — and the pounds just fell off.

When the night of the party finally arrived, I felt strangely shy.

The dress fitted me like a glove. I must admit I cheated a little with a girdle but, having said that, I managed to wedge myself into the frock without much difficulty.

"You look beautiful, Judith," Jenny said when I arrived at the party.

"Thank you," I said loftily, feeling anything but beautiful.

"There's someone I want you to meet," she whispered, eyes bright.

"Please, Jenny, spare me your matchmaking!" I hissed, and fled to the nearest dark corner, where I skulked for ages.

"Would you care to dance?" A voice broke through my unhappy thoughts.

I lifted my face and looked into the kindest, warmest, bluest eyes I've ever seen in my life.

I opened my mouth to decline, as I couldn't dance to save my life and no way was I going to make a fool of myself in front of everybody . . .

"I'd love to," I was astonished to hear myself say instead and, before I knew it, his arm was around my waist and I was stumbling around the dance floor with him, repeatedly treading on his toes.

He seemed rather tense and anxious — still, I understood. He was doing his duty, prodded, no doubt, by Jenny.

He twirled me around and I promptly ground his foot into the floor with my high heel. He winced and said, "Do you mind if we sit down?"

"I think we'd better," I sighed. "Before I cripple you for life!"

"Oh, it's not that," he told me quickly. "It's me. I tire easily. You see, I was in a bad car accident last year and I'm still recuperating really. I'm sorry, I'm not much fun."

What was going on? This man had transported me to Heaven and he was apologising to me!

I presumed he was about to dump me. After all, who actually wants to dance with Nelly the Elephant gone crazy?

Gently, he escorted me to a chaise-longue and said, "I'll get us both a drink and something to eat. What would you like?"

A bucket of soup, a pan of fried potatoes, half a buttered loaf and a big wedge of chocolate cake, I felt like screaming out.

"Just a slimmers' tonic," I said meekly.

HE had no sooner departed than Jen swooped down on me."Well, now, you two seem to be getting along great," she stated with glee, and my happiness went out like an exploding light bulb.

So help me, I thought, if she'd put him up to it, I'd swing for her!

I glared at her and hissed, "It was only a dance, Jenny, that's all. Please don't make anything more of it. I don't even know the man."

"His name's Paul Brewster." She lowered her voice. "He's one of the nicest men I know and he's had a bad time.

"He lost his wife in a car accident last year and he was in hospital for eight long months, his injuries were so very bad."

"How old is he?" I couldn't help wondering.

"Thirty-odd." She shrugged evasively.

"How many odds?" I demanded, suspicions growing.

"A few months," she mumbled.

He was just a boy — a mere boy, I thought!

"Go away, Jenny!" I muttered between clenched teeth.

She slunk away.

Paul came back with a tray sagging with goodies. My eyes lit up.

"Tuck in," he said cheerfully. "I like a woman with an appetite."

Mine suddenly vanished. "I'm on a diet," I confessed miserably.

"You look fine to me." He eyed me appreciatively. "I loathe skinny women."

So, thank you, God. You send me a saint — unfortunately he's seven years too young!

"You sound like my mother." I forced a smile. "She's done everything but inject me with cream cakes!"

"Here!" He thrust a plate at me and smiled.

And that was the ice well and truly broken for us.

We talked throughout the whole of the party. Oh, I tried to remain cool and indifferent, but he was such a nice man — and I really liked him.

He was the first man I had ever met with whom I'd felt so at ease.

And then there were his wonderful, friendly eyes.

He offered to see me home and, in agonies of embarrassment, I found myself accepting.

At the gate, I gushed, "Thank you for seeing me home. It's been lovely. Really it has. Thank you. Goodnight, er, yes, thank you."

I fled into the house like a scalded cat.

EARLY next morning, Mother burst into my bedroom."Get up, Judith!" she commanded. "That man was on the phone for you."

I sat bolt upright in bed and squeaked, "What man?"

"What man?" she snorted. "How many do you know? Paul Brewster, that's what man. He wanted to take you out for lunch and I said yes. He's picking you up at eleven."

"Mother!" I gasped. "You had no right!"

"Now, you listen to me, Judith." She plonked herself down on my bed and my heart sank. She was in the throes of her Mother Knows Best rôle.

"Do you want to go through life alone?" she demanded. "Because that's what will happen if you don't make an effort. Believe me, he's a nice man — I know!

"How many other men do you think are going to ask you out?

"You're heading towards forty, Judith, and good men are thin on the ground."

I glared at her. It was typical of Mother to remind me of my age.

"It was very lucky you happened to meet!" she added for emphasis.

"Luck had nothing to do with it!" I snorted. "It was Jen."

"Whatever!" Mother shrugged. "It makes no difference. He likes you. So go to lunch and enjoy yourself for once."

"Which tent do you suggest I wear?" I asked tartly.

"The blue," she replied, without batting an eyelid.

HOW can I describe those next few months? Divine? Confusing? Happy? Wonderful? All of those. I only know that he would keep calling for me and I would keep going out with him.

Every night, I would lie in bed and promise myself that I wouldn't see him again.

But, the next evening, he would knock on the door and, when I saw him standing hopefully on the step, my foolish heart always got the better of my senses.

Then, one Sunday afternoon, as we strolled aimlessly through the park, he suddenly said, "Did Jenny tell you about the accident, Judith?"

"A little," I confessed.

"Did she tell you I was driving when it happened?" He turned to me.

"No," I said carefully. "She never mentioned that."

"Well, I was." He stared bleakly ahead. "I lost control of the car on a patch of ice and there hasn't been a day gone by that I haven't thought — If only . . .

"But nothing will change the fact that I was responsible for Claire's death."

"It was an accident, Paul," I said gently.

"Oh, I was cleared of all blame at the inquest," he went on quite tonelessly. "But I wonder . . . I'll always wonder. I lay in hospital for eight months, going over and over it in my mind.

"I still have nightmares when I wake up shouting and sweating. I want you to know that. I want you to know exactly what you could be letting yourself in for."

He turned to me then, taking my hands in his.

I held my breath.

"When I was in hospital," he said softly, "I used to wish that I'd die. But somehow I carried on living — well, going through the motions, anyway. Trying to pick up the pieces.

"And then I met you and, suddenly, there was someone, something, a reason to get up in the morning.

"I never thought I'd say this to another woman, Judith, but I love you. I think I fell in love with you the minute I saw you standing in the corner at David's party.

"I understood you without knowing you. You were like me — hiding away in a corner. I could see myself in you." He smiled gently.

"If you'll have me, I want us to get married."

"I'm older than you," I said through dry lips.

"What's age got to do with anything?" Wonderful eyes gazed down into mine. "It won't alter the way I feel about you. Nothing will ever change that.

"Since I met you, I've started to live — and love — again."

"No!" I tried to pull away, but he held on. "I'm sorry. Seven years! It's too much . . . and I'm . . . no, I'm sorry, Paul!"

"If you don't care for me, just say so," he said gently. "But please don't use silly excuses. There's no need. I understand. I'm no Mel Gibson."

"You are to me," I whispered.

"Really?"

His eyes held mine and I nodded before asking tremulously, "Will it work? You and me, I mean."

"Oh, yes." He drew me carefully into his arms. "It'll work. You'll see. We're two of a kind. Both a little lonely, both a little lost and afraid. But together, we can conquer the world."

"You idiot!" I leaned against him, sniffing happily. "It takes me all my time to hoist myself on to a bus . . . and you talk about conquering the world."

"Ah, but from now on I'll be there to lend a helping hand."

His eyes twinkled. "I'll make sure you don't miss that bus — I'll give you a gentle shove if necessary."

Our eyes met and we burst out laughing.

"You want a broken hand?" I inquired archly.

"Better than a broken heart any day!" he replied gallantly.

"I'll stick to my diet," I promised. "And, by the time we're married, I'll be the kind of woman who can run around in the shower and not get wet."

"I'd rather you stayed as you are," he murmured, to my delight. "Big- hearted and cuddly."

"Ah, well, looks like I've got myself a toy boy!" I sighed, eyes shining.

"We're going to laugh a lot, Judith," he promised, beaming at me.

"Yes," I smiled. "I think we are."

THE way Mother carried on you'd think nobody had ever got married before.

It was exactly the same five months after the wedding when I found out I was expecting.

Mother suddenly became an expert on pregnancy.

"Our mother, the gynaecologist!" I said to Jenny, and she grinned and warned, "You'd better be careful, Judith. Mother might want to deliver the baby herself!"

I shuddered and we giggled.

"Oh, Jenny." I covered her hand with mine. "I owe you so much. If it hadn't been for your matchmaking, Paul and I might never have met."

She turned horribly red and shifty-eyed, then blurted out, "Actually, Judith, Paul wasn't who I had in mind for you that night. Of course, when I saw you getting on so well with him I was thrilled."

"Not Paul?" I echoed, amazed. "Who, then?"

"Bernard Hurst," she mumbled guiltily.

"Bernard Hurst!" I shrieked. "Well, thank you, Jenny! I wasn't that desperate!"

She looked so crestfallen, like a naughty child. And I loved her so! I hugged her and, relieved, she hugged me back. Best of friends, best of sisters.

Well, I did it — I gave birth to twin girls, no less. Two babies in one fell swoop! We were over the moon!

When Paul and I were finally alone, and, believe you me, Mother had to be dragged away protesting, I said tentatively, "I've been thinking, Paul, if you don't mind, I'd like to name one of the girls Claire."

There was such a long silence that even the busy ward seemed quiet.

"Do you know," he said eventually, "that you're a wonderful woman? Big in every sense of the word?"

"Please!" I shuddered. "Don't remind me!"

"I didn't mean that."

"I know what you meant."

Our eyes met.

"I love you."

"I love you, too!"

He kissed me and murmured, "I think I'm the happiest man alive today."

"Me, too!" I sighed dreamily.

"You're not a man!" he quipped.

"Go home, Paul!" I giggled. "I'll see you later."

At the door, he turned, looking suddenly lost and forlorn and making my heart flip over as he said, "I can't wait for you to come home. I miss you already, Judith. It's a cold house without you."

"I'll be home tomorrow," I reminded him, blowing him a kiss.

When he had gone, I lay back against the pillows, thinking of the next days, of all the days to come, days just waiting to be filled with love and all kinds of good things.

All those tomorrows . . . the ones I'd once thought would never be mine. ■

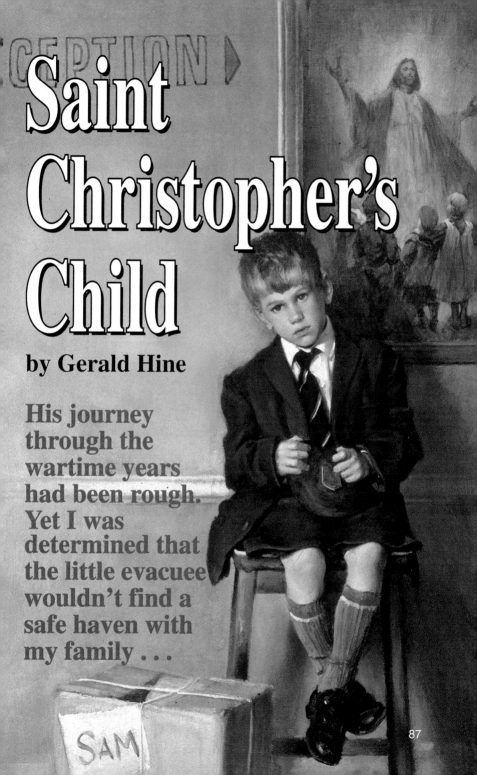

Saint Christopher's Child

by Gerald Hine

His journey through the wartime years had been rough. Yet I was determined that the little evacuee wouldn't find a safe haven with my family . . .

I WAS checking the fence at the top of the orchard when the child came towards me, leaping like a fawn through the clumps of tall grass. It was Harold's grandson, Tony.

He called to me when he got nearer and the glare of the strong sun played tricks with my eyes.

His face . . . it was the same . . . and the shiny, blond hair was the same, too.

Somehow, now became then, as fifty years melted away and I was transported back to a house with a higgledy-piggledy roof and tiny leaded windows. I could almost see the old, smoke-blackened forge.

I thought once more of Harold and suddenly became a boy again . . .

Harold arrived on a misty morning in mid-November, among a group of silent children, bumbling from an old Bedford bus, which still smoked and groaned in protest after its long climb up to the village schoolroom.

"Where are they from?" I heard Mrs Catley ask. "They be skinny little devils."

Mrs Catley was from Babwell Farm and was round and plump like her healthy family.

"Now, ladies," Mrs Phelps, the Rector's wife remonstrated, "give the children a little room!"

She may as well have addressed the cows looking over the hawthorn hedge, for the "ladies" all surged forward into the school, in a jumble of arms, legs and evacuees caught underfoot.

My mother turned then and, unfortunately, saw me.

"Home," she ordered. "If you get in there, it'll be bedlam!"

My mum never expected the best of me. She was Welsh-born and, when she flew into a temper, Dad and I would keep very silent.

"Sit tight, lad," he would always say. "It's only a ten-second blaster."

When I got home that day, Mum had a rabbit stew on the hob, and the smell of it almost took my breath away. Our kitchen took up almost the whole house and there were only two bedrooms.

One was really a landing with stairs leading up to it. That was where I slept.

It was a big step down into the kitchen from my room. In the kitchen there was a table where the washing things were kept.

It was on this table that I was put to be scrubbed each day. It was agony, but my mum was a stickler for cleanliness.

The area by the fire was the sitting place, where we spent the winter evenings toasting our knees, with thick woollies protecting our backs against draughts.

Mum and Dad each had a big wooden chair with high arms and a cushion on the seat.

In the corner by the big oven, was my chair.

When I arrived home, I sat in the window watching the hill.

My mum had an inbuilt mechanism that seemed to accelerate her movements in times of stress. Now, she came charging down the lane like a steam train, with a sickly-looking child clinging to her hand.

He looked like an animated stick insect, as his spindly legs struggled to keep up.

Once in the kitchen, he stood, obviously very nervous, clutching a paper carrier bag.

There were rings of grime around his eyes and neck. His hair seemed stiff and tangled, and he scratched at it in an absent-minded way.

His sharp face was pinched and grey and he had enormous cow eyes, brown and liquid, which peered out in a sombre way under long, curved lashes.

Brought up under the shadow of the scrubbing brush, I found his appearance hard to take in!

I HADN'T wanted anyone to come, as I wasn't used to other children at home.

"It's the war," everyone said, but the war seemed so remote to us, just words coming out of the wireless.

It was said that children were in danger because of bombs and things. But, I ask you, was it my fault if they lived in stupid places?

I had mulled it over for days before getting used to the idea. Eventually, I accepted that another boy was coming to live with us, but I didn't have to like him, did I?

Then, this disaster — I hadn't even got a proper boy!

I felt cheated and knew, from that first moment, that I hated him.

Dad came in then and, without saying anything, lifted down the zinc bath, filling both the big kettles.

Then Dad took off Harold's clothes and threw them out into the wood shed.

Harold sat rigid in the bath, clutching at the sides until his knuckles strained like knots.

The carrier bag contained no other clothes at all.

"What's he going to wear?" I asked. "He can't have my clothes!"

Mum grabbed me by the shoulder and her angry shake made my teeth rattle.

In my bedroom, I selected the most tattered garments I could find, and a shrunken pair of socks, all lumpy with darning.

After the ordeal of his bath, Harold looked quite different. His pale skin looked all pink and glowing now, and his hair had turned into a shiny blond colour.

Mum lifted him out and dried him off, talking to him quietly, telling him what a good boy he was and how he would soon get used to us.

He'll not get used to me, I vowed, noticing how she gave him an affectionate squeeze, before wrapping him in a warm towel and putting him on . . .

"That's my chair!" I yelled "Why does he have to sit on my chair?"

Mum gave me a warning look. "Oh, you great baby!"

But I couldn't stop the tears. Didn't I matter any more? I just bubbled, and Harold watched from the folds of his towel.

Mum threw a cloth on the table then, while I sulkily got out the knives and forks. I had my own place by Dad.

At the table, Harold shoved down rabbit stew as though his life depended on it, followed by a huge apple dumpling, forced in until his cheeks bulged.

"Nobody's going to take the food off you, lad," Mum told him gently. "You can always have some more."

"More?" Harold echoed incredulously. "Cor!"

Harold didn't stir from my chair all day and, at one point, I thought I might pitch him out of it — but Mum was watching me like a hawk.

He was put to bed at six o'clock — in my spare pair of pyjamas, of course! He was fast asleep when I went up.

After a few minutes, I crept down to the bottom of the stairs. I could sit there behind the door and keep up with all the village gossip.

"I thought they were coming from London?" my dad was saying.

"No, Portsmouth — right off the docks!"

"But a boy like Harold, for pity's sake! Why did you choose him?"

"I had to, Stan — nobody seemed to know who he was. I just couldn't come home and leave him there."

"Tom doesn't think much of him."

"Oh, bless him. It'll make him realise how lucky he is."

Lucky! I ran back and buried my head in the pillow. If losing your clothes and your place and being yelled at was lucky, I dreaded my next stroke of good fortune.

HAROLD was standing in an enamel bowl being washed again when I went down to the kitchen next morning.

"Eat your breakfast quickly," Mum ordered, "or you'll be late for school."

"What about him?"

"I'm not sending him today."

I threw down my spoon, splattering porridge across the oilcloth. "You mean I've got to go and he's going to stop here messing with my things?"

Ominously, Mum moved towards me, leaving Harold to shiver.

"I'm running out of patience with you, Tom. Get your clothes on and out of that door before I help you on your way!"

Six of the other evacuees came to school that morning. The boys were a bit cheeky, so all us village children played wild horses and charged round knocking them out of the way, just to warn them that they'd better be careful.

I lost my place next to my special friend, Margaret Grey, and I heard Mrs Ross checking off the other names . . . apparently Harold was to sit next to Margaret! Was there to be no end to it?

Now I had to sit next to a skinny ginger-nut with spots. She was called Mattie and she looked at me as though I had crawled out of the nearest pigsty.

Harold sat huddled in my chair when I flew in from school. There was no-one else in the kitchen and I had him off it in a second.

"And keep off," I warned, showing him my fist. "And out of my way."

The warning wasn't necessary — he crept about the place like a ghost. The only flicker of interest he displayed was when Mum called us to the table.

His eating was usually accompanied by awed whispers. "Puddin' — cor," or, "Cake — cor."

And the following days weren't easy, either. Harold was never told off. It was easy to see why, of course — he never did anything, apart from eat.

I, on the other hand, came in for the whole lot! I got groused at for not speaking to him properly and my thighs smarted from the time I got caught reminding him whose house it was!

Bedtime was better, because I had him on his own. Once, I sat on his head until he turned a very interesting shade of purple!

Going to school was pretty good as well. I positively encouraged the others to pick on Harold, too.

★ ★ ★ ★

But things change.

As the weeks went by, baiting Harold became less fun and, eventually, I realised why.

He never complained or showed any reaction. I'd never seen him cry, not even when I'd really tormented him. And he never split on me to my parents.

Funnily enough, he didn't keep out of my way, either. He was always there, ready for his next helping of trouble, almost as though he, well, liked me.

I knew that couldn't be true, but, whatever, I sort of got used to him being around.

In early December, I got my chair back when Dad found another. Now Harold and I could sit facing each other across the fireplace.

Sometimes, I would mouth rude words across to him to see what he would do, but he never came out of his trance.

It was strange having Harold there at Christmas, too. We always put up paper trimmings and had a tree with real candles.

We both had stockings, although I watched pretty closely to make sure he didn't get more presents than I did.

Strangely, there was no word from his family, and no presents.

In bed on Christmas night, I woke up bursting for the toilet, as I'd drunk masses of pop. The house was quiet and there was just enough light to see that Harold's bed was empty.

I went down to the kitchen. Harold had lit every candle on the Christmas tree and it blazed and glittered in the darkness like something alive.

I was mesmerised and Harold knelt, huddled in rapture, with his bony feet sticking out behind him, blue with cold.

I don't know how long he'd been there but my joy shrank when I saw the candle grease dripping from twig to twig.

Harold looked up. "Do you think Jesus really loves us?" he asked intently.

"Don't expect he loves me much!" I said roughly. "And, Harold, we'll have to move quick, or the house will burn down!"

I didn't tell anyone what Harold had done. Instead, I gathered all the candle holders and put them back in the box. I don't know, he'd looked so, so . . .

Anyway, I just let it go.

A LONG, wet spring dribbled into a reluctant summer. Mum actually came near to losing patience with Harold, who kept picking huge bunches of wet primroses and bluebells and taking them in to her, where they dripped all over the flagstones and made them slippery.

We were glad when the sun started to shine.

I'd reached the stage where I now tolerated Harold. I still hated him, of course, just for being there — but found myself looking round for him if he was out of sight for long.

The astonishing thing was that people seemed to like him.

Mrs Thomas from the Council Houses, who wouldn't allow me past her gate, gave him a jam tart one morning for no reason at all. He'd changed a lot, too. The grey colour of his skin had long gone and his constant eating had fattened his spindly arms and legs.

His face had altered as well and his hair was shining with health.

That was another thing — he was always running about now.

And he got on well at school, considering he knew practically nothing when he came.

Harold still sat next to Margaret Grey and I bitterly resented that. I knew that she helped him and my pique flared into rage later in the summer term when they were given a project to do together.

It was all a bit silly because Margaret didn't want to ditch me. Eventually we ended up as a trio and it didn't seem at all odd.

The summer holidays finally arrived and Margaret went off to stay with her grandparents in Weymouth.

One day, we sat up in a tree throwing pebbles into a cocoa tin. "Why don't nobody ever come to see you?" I ventured pleasantly. "Can't they stand the sight of your ugly chops?"

Harold gripped his pebble and didn't answer. "Mam's too busy," he said eventually.

"Shouldn't think she was very busy with you!" I declared.

Harold frowned. "You don't know about it. Sometimes she would fall over when she came home. Other times, her men friends would come with her late and I'd get pushed outside."

"Outside? Wow-ee!" My mind soared. "I'll bet you had some fun."

The liquid eyes clouded. "No," he said dismally. "Once, I stopped out for days and no-one came for me."

THAT weekend, Harold did something totally out of character. He climbed up on to the roof of the forge to look at the remains of a bird's nest.

Getting up, he dislodged umpteen tiles then, at the ridge, lost his footing and brought half the chimney down with him.

We ran out and found him dangling from a hook which had caught in the back of his jumper.

Mum exploded into a really super blaster and he was dragged indoors and finally introduced to the slapped thighs treatment.

"You could have killed yourself!" she raved in her anxiety.

Harold hopped about clutching his legs and then the silent boy, who had shown not a shred of emotion in all the months, started to cry.

It was a masterpiece! He choked and howled and shrieked, with the tears spouting like a spray.

He crouched against the sideboard, his thin shoulders racked with convulsive sobs, and gradually sank on to the floor.

It started to upset me, but he pushed aside all my attempts to help and crawled under the big table where a medley of coughs, sniffs and sobs continued unabated until dinner time.

At one o'clock, Mum, rather anxiously, said, "Dinner's on the table." And we waited.

The fringe of the cloth stirred and a face peered sheepishly out with knuckles rubbing at red eyes. Harold climbed into his place, gave us all a shy smile and proceeded to eat enough to keep the British Army for a week!

I didn't understand such things, but something had happened to Harold far beyond the effects of physical discomfort.

The tension seemed to go out of him and he became . . . a person.

Now that he wasn't so jittery, he was very interesting to talk to. Having lived near the docks, he knew a lot about cargo ships and about the big, naval craft that regularly called there. One night, he had sneaked on to a destroyer and looked down the gun barrels!

I didn't realise it at the time but that was my best ever summer. Whatever we did, there were two of us and it made life a whole lot better.

But, of course, I had to spoil things. Without fail, just when the world looked good, I would say or do something that would bring the sky down on my head.

We'd had real fun on my birthday. Mum had made a cake and we salvaged twelve candles to go on it.

Being a Thursday, the ice-cream cart came. But, instead of a penny cornet, we had a whole pile of ice-cream with jelly and tinned fruit.

We'd sat on either side of the fireplace listening to ITMA on the wireless and threatening each other with the hearth brushes and shouting, "Can I do you now, sir?" at the top of our voices until we were hoarse.

The following day, I'd missed Harold for maybe an hour, and eventually found him sitting cross-legged right at the top of the orchard.

HE was looking at a small, bronze medallion. Coming close behind him, I recognised it as a St Christopher medal.

Quite suddenly, I had to have it and snatched it away. Normally, he never offered any resistance, so his bare fury took me completely by surprise.

He sprang up and threw himself at me.

The medal went up in the air and disappeared. Harold scratched at the turf, then turned back to me, shaking with rage.

We went at it like two ferrets in a bag, over and over, punching and scratching. I felt his nails rake my neck like knives, but slewed him round and got a good crack to his eye.

I tried to hold his neck but his bony knuckles twice split my mouth and I tasted the blood. In desperation, I brought my knee up under his ribs, but he came back, head down, taking all my breath and making the whole world red.

I felt someone grab my collar and, the next moment, I was flailing thin air. Harold, in my father's other hand, looked like a demented puppet.

Back indoors, very little was said. Mum dabbed at Harold's puffy eye while Dad just shoved my head into a bucket of freezing water and told me to swill out my mouth.

He was very angry. When I tried to speak, he wouldn't listen. "I don't want excuses," he said, pushing my head back into the bucket. "You got what was due to you."

I so much wanted to say something to Harold that night. I wished it hadn't happened and I needed to tell him. But the words just wouldn't come. Sleep did instead.

I WOKE late the next morning. The sun was shining on to Harold's empty bed.

I dived down the stairs with my pyjamas flapping. I knew something was wrong as soon as I saw Dad sitting there in his good trousers.

"Harold's gone," he said.

"But why?" I implored, climbing on to his knee.

"I think you know why. It didn't work, did it?"

"Oh, Dad."

"We knew you gave him a rough time, but it seemed to sort itself out — 'til yesterday. We can't put up with that."

I went outside and sat on the bank. The grass soaked my pyjamas but I didn't even feel it. The guilt overwhelmed me. Harold had never asked for anything, or tried to push me out.

I'd just hated him because he had been small and timid — yes, and because my mother had cuddled him when he was frightened.

When he had grown strong and turned into a friend, I'd been too stupid even to notice. It was myself I should hate.

Where had he gone? Did they know he needed tons to eat?

He told me once he'd been out for days and no-one had bothered about it. Well, I'd bother when I found out where he was.

I pleaded, but they wouldn't tell me. I could put up with them being angry with me, but this went deeper. I couldn't make them understand that, whatever they felt, I felt even worse.

The days dragged on. It was like being the only person in the world.

THEN, one day, I saw the letter. It was only a glimpse before it was snatched away. St Andrew's House. I knew what that was! It was a Council Home!

My cousin Ivy went to school in Wincanton with someone from there.

I didn't know what I could do if I went, but I had to go.

Twice, I walked to the bike shed and back again, until, finally, I found the courage and pedalled off down the road.

St Andrew's House was a murky-grey building with a high stone wall all round it.

My stomach gripped itself into an agonising knot. Getting over the wall was no problem, but what next?

All the windows were shut except one. I went round and round the building, running past the big, carved door and twisting in and out of the bushes.

It just didn't occur to me to bang on the door and simply ask if Harold was there.

It would have to be that window!

I scrambled up the creeper, knuckles grinding against the wall, until I was level with the opening, then I leapt sideways.

The net curtain blinded me as I went through, but the noise upon landing was shattering and crockery flew in all directions.

Gaping, incredulous faces watched my swash-buckling entrance. To my horror, the room was full of girls in various stages of getting their clothes on!

Pandemonium broke out and I ran. People and children rushed in from every direction. I bounced off a great fat woman in a white cap and fled up an empty passage.

Footsteps pounded down the passage and I shot through the half-open doorway and under a bed.

Someone was sitting on the other side of the bed with his feet dangling — I knew instinctively the feet belonged to Harold.

I stood up as the mob charged through the door.

With tears stinging my eyes, I twisted my arms around the metal of the bedhead and screeched over and over again, "Let Harold go! Please send him home!"

I remember the hands dragging at me and Harold trying to cling on to my arms. They got me out, of course, and sent me home in a police car with my bike sticking out of the boot.

Nobody punished me, though. I couldn't help wishing they would — it might have made me feel better.

Yet it was all for nothing. There was no hope now — Harold had gone.

One day, they would send him back to where he had come from, where nobody wanted him, and I had never even told him that I didn't hate him any more.

It took me three days to find his St Christopher medal . . . His bed was still in my room and I hung it from the centre rail where it would have been right over his head.

Next morning, I was sent to Gillingham to do some shopping. It was a funny morning. I wasn't normally entrusted with lists and money, other than to take to the village shop.

When I came back down the hill, my front brake squealing and the bag wobbling on my handlebars, I had the strangest feeling.

Nothing I had bought was really needed. I'd just been got out of the way.

But why?

Perhaps they were going to get rid of me, too. If I were them, I'd want to get rid of me!

HAROLD was sitting in his own chair by the hearth when I got home. When we sat at the tea-table, I felt my grin ticking my earlobes and Harold blushed quite pink as he wolfed down his third piece of cake.

It was good to see him sitting there!

Mum tucked us into our beds and even Dad came up to say goodnight.

The moon filtered through the small, leaded panes and made a dim pattern on Harold's bed as he lay looking up at his medal.

Words came more easily in the dark.

"Harold?"

"Yes."

"Where did you get it?"

"A man — saw him three times. Only thing I ever did have."

Rain started to patter on the porch outside.

"Tom?"

"Yes."

"My mam's dead — from the bombs. They told Dad this morning — your dad, I mean."

"Are you upset?"

"A bit. I think. I dunno!"

"You'll have to stop here, then."

"D'you think I could?"

" 'Course! And he can be your dad, too, if you like."

That was how it came about that Harold and I grew up like two brothers, in the brown forge cottage under the hill.

He became the first boy from the village school ever to pass the eleven-plus examination.

There was something in him — an insatiable thirst for knowledge, a restlessness — which drove him around the world as a brilliant engineer.

I often thought of his precious Saint Christopher medal.

Harold's way wasn't my way. I was a country boy through and through, content to drag my father's business into a changing world.

Harold married Margaret one Christmas of long ago when real candles spluttered on the tree.

I envied him nothing, and learned from him the need to search one's own soul before judging any human being.

Margaret and my Mattie were in the garden with young Tony scampering around their legs.

Harold broke away and came towards me, smiling. I hadn't seen him for 15 years and we talked, at first, almost like strangers.

On impulse, I asked, "Do you remember when you first came here?"

"Like yesterday."

"Those first months I was a pig to you."

Harold looked astonished, then laughed. "I didn't think you'd ever realised the truth.

"From that first day, I idolised you! You were my hero — fearless, never afraid of trouble!"

"Too thick to see it coming, more like," I chipped in, suddenly embarrassed.

"I was determined to be strong like you. I couldn't do it physically, so I studied like mad."

"You were strong enough when we had our fight."

Harold's face was a study. "What a disaster that was! But I knew you would come to the Home for me, Tom."

Amazed, I realised I had always underestimated the wisdom of Harold . . . ■

THE COLLIE

**A poem by Joyce Stranger,
inspired by an illustration
by Mark Viney**

The best collie I had was a bit of a nut.
We had to make sure that all doors were shut,
Or she herded the horses out of their stalls,
She gathered the hens against the barn walls.
She drove the ducks away from the pool,
She herded the children as they went to school.
She herded the sheep, a joy to behold
But always insisted they go in the fold.
One wintry day she startled us all.
We knew the cattle were locked in their stall.
The sky was black and the snow lay deep.
Safe in fields by the house were all the sheep.
Beth found herself with nothing to do,
But herd she must, (this story is true).
I'd failed to secure the big barn latch.
She butted the door and released the catch.
The penned up cattle were glad to be out.
Away through the snow . . .
Then I heard a shout.
The cowman had found the empty barn,
Had taken his dog and raised the alarm.
For several miles we followed their tracks

Through driving storm till we saw their backs.
There were the cattle in deepening snow
Beth guarding them proudly, her eyes aglow.
Back to the barn she happily went
When her charges were in, she was content.
Now the door's fast latched and the cattle, I know,
Are safely warm and out of the snow.
No harm was done but that's not the way
To spend one's time on a bitter day.
Now Beth is old and by the fire does sleep
And only in dreams does she herd her sheep.

On This Enchanted Shore

by Angela Noel

*Here, long ago,
I'd let happiness slip through
my fingers like sand. But now I
was back, and time was standing still . . .*

IT'S the evenings I remember best. We loved to sit on this bare sandy shore as the day slipped away, taking the visitors with it. Tonight, the water still rustles and ripples like silk as the waves lap the shore and the last birds fall silent.

The shadows are lengthening now and a salty breeze ruffles the spiky grass on the top of the dunes as the sea starts to turn pink and yellow in the low sun of an autumn evening.

How often I have stood here in reminiscence and how I have dreamed of seeing it one more time!

Not far away there are green cliffs where we loved to ride and rocky caves we scrambled around in for hours. But this stretch of seashore has remained with me as our special place.

One of us would await the other here when work was over, and the tiredness of a hectic day would melt away as our hearts and minds fused again.

Yet still I'm not sure whether this holiday is a mistake. Everything is as I have remembered it a thousand times — except that now I stand here alone.

I should have realised the past is another country and I took a one-way ticket out.

I can never be eighteen again and Peter can never be twenty.

I wonder where he is living now . . . Does he even remember my name any more, I wonder.

Of course, I don't regret anything — neither leaving him nor loving him — I don't think. No, we were too young, too immature to make lasting choices, but it was a truly unforgettable episode in my life.

Peter was working happily at a little lakeside café that year, not caring that his future was hazy; he was Mr Easy-Going.

He used to tell me about his parents, both successful theatre people, both moody, intense, frenetic. He came here to escape.

He loved this quiet beach, he loved that sweet summer — and he loved me.

Oh yes, for a few timeless months that summer it was the real thing, for both of us.

In contrast to Peter, I was brimming with plans. My job in a nearby hotel was only temporary, a rather boring means to scrape together a few hundred pounds to supplement my grant before I went to university.

There, I had decided, I would gain an amazingly good honours degree that would be my gateway to an outstanding career in something prestigious — like law.

I used to pose on a rock and expound to an invisible jury until, laughing and yet meaning it, Peter would pull me down, saying, "Don't act like that, Abigail, don't ever act!"

One night, here on the shore, we seemed so close that I actually confided in him that I visualised some Mr Rich-and-Handsome, probably a renowned or at least up-and-coming barrister, bursting on to my scene. Peter said nothing.

I was as restless as Peter was settled, as ambitious as he was content. How could we be happy together? Yet for one summer, we were just that.

M Y reverie is disturbed. I can hear someone else on the beach, a steady crunching of feet on the wet sand.

The light is fading. All I can see is a hazy silhouette as it draws nearer; the figure of a man, scarf flicking in the breeze.

I begin to walk away along the shore, a little feeling of tightness starting inside me.

I quicken my pace, stumbling here and there on the soft sand. Faintly, between my own footfalls, I hear his, following me. Also quickening.

Faster still. The beach seems to stretch forever. Why is there no-one else in sight?

His feet are really hurrying now, growing closer.

"Abigail? Abigail?"

I suppress a cry. I can't have heard my own name. It's all in my mind — yet the voice sounds familiar . . .

I look over my shoulder, wary and yet mesmerised. And suddenly I'm falling, my feet caught up in some driftwood. The shore rushes up to meet me and all the breath is knocked from my body. "Abigail, it is you, isn't it? Are you all right? Here, give me your hand. It was my fault, I'm sorry I startled you —"

He looked apologetic. "When I saw your outline against the water it seemed impossible, and yet I was so sure it was you."

"Peter!" That's all I can say, just "Peter!"

"I never meant to frighten you."

"I'm not in the least frightened!" I retort, furious with myself and lying frantically. "What are you doing here, Abigail?"

I get to my feet. "I've got a week's holiday," I explain matter-of-factly. "I thought it might be nice to look up the old place after all this time".

How convincingly I manage to hide the hours of hesitation spent wondering whether I could bear to sit by the shore again, to face up to the myriad of memories it would bring back.

He puts his hands on my arms and we face each other in the fading daylight. How often we stood this way all those years ago!

"Oh, Abigail, it's great to see you again!"

"It must be what — six or seven years?" I ask casually, not revealing that I know exactly how long it is to the day since the last time we met.

"Is it as long as that? Looking at you now it seems like yesterday."

He smiles and it is reflected in his lightened voice. I could close my eyes and listen to that voice the way one might listen to Beethoven.

"Let's go back to the café, Abigail. I want to look at you properly."

My eyes widen. "You still work at that place? What was it called?" I rack my brains, dredging through old memories before exclaiming, "'The Water's Edge', that's it!"

Once I'd have said it with scorn but the years have taught me much and now I'm only grateful if, miraculously, he hasn't changed.

How wonderful if everything could be the same just for this one precious week!

THE café has changed. It's shut up for the night, of course, but even in the growing dark I can see that it's grown from the little wooden shack where we first met.

Peter produces keys and goes in ahead of me, flicking on lights. Blinking in the sudden brightness, I stand open-mouthed in astonishment.

Gone is the small, dingy shack with Formica surfaces. The main room is huge, airy, cheerful and impeccably furnished with old wooden tables, posies of fresh flowers and nautical wall decorations of ropes and anchors.

"Like it?"

"I can't believe it!" My gaze swings back to Peter. He is older, naturally, and the high-cheeked face is a little fuller, but the boyish smile remains.

The familiar lines that I used to trace with my fingers are a little deeper now, but still there, and the humorous light still flickers in his brown eyes.

He makes two coffees and we sit on high stools beside the bar.

"Tell me what you're doing these days, Abi."

"I'm with a firm of solicitors."

"In London?"

"No, still in Birmingham."

"You got that degree in law, then?"

"Nothing worked out quite the way I intended," I admit, avoiding his searching gaze.

"No Mr Rich-and-Handsome, Q.C.?"

I hesitate, wanting to keep my pride intact — but he's watching me, not teasing now but serious. His are not eyes one can lie to.

"There was someone for a while." For too long, I think bitterly. "Let's just call him Mr Rich-and-Ruthless, and talk about you instead."

"But you are a solicitor now?"

"No, a secretary and P.A. to one. It wasn't what I planned but I really do enjoy it."

Even so, I feel my anger begin to burn again at the memory of how I quit my degree course for that other man, stupid me, and how I thought a bit of charm, an assured manner with waiters and a Gold Card equalled Mr Right.

It took me two whole years to grow up enough to admit to myself that, frankly, he was just Mr Big Mistake.

Peter, remembering my grand plans, has tactfully changed the subject and is telling me of some small incident today involving twin toddlers who bewitched and confused everyone and my mind swings right back to the present.

Is he married now, I wonder, does he have children of his own? Instead, I ask after his parents.

He presses his lips together. "Split up, I'm afraid."

"Oh Peter, I'm so sorry!"

He sighs. "It may not be a permanent split. They've done it before. That's the kind of people they are. Over-emotional. Everything has to be played out as a melodrama."

"Perhaps they enjoy life that way, all blacks and whites, no dull greys."

"That's them exactly!" A shake of his head. "Not the sort of marriage I want, though."

"You're not married, then?" I try to steady my voice. Selfish of me, of course. I ought to wish him well, but somehow the thought of him with a wife is a picture I just can't face.

"No, I not married. It's not something I've really thought about."

I feel I have to make an excuse for asking. "It's just that this place seems to have a woman's touch."

Peter glances around. "I employ good staff."

"Oh, you're the manager here now?"

Peter's eyes crease ironically, and that old endearing smile twitches the corners of his mouth. "Go on, Abigail, admit it! You were thinking, 'What a boring, unambitious creature he is, still in the same old café'!"

"But it's far from being the same old café," I protest. "It's really something now. As for the rest, you could never be boring — and unambitious? Well, cliché though it may be, I've found out money isn't

104

everything."

There is a sweet silence while Peter puts some more coffee on, then he turns to me with a thoughtful expression and says, "Of course, you were right, Abi, I couldn't spend my whole life just being a dogsbody in a small café."

"So how did you set this up?"

"I took out a loan, bought the place from my boss when he retired and started improving it. After I'd rebuilt this one, I opened another one further along the coast and I have plans for a couple more."

"I should have guessed," I tell him, realising he's done what I always believed he was capable of — he's carved out a good business.

So we have both changed. Perhaps it would have been better simply to keep the memories of good times past.

"But . . .?" he prompts.

I looked up questioningly.

"You seem to have reservations, Abigail. I thought you'd approve." Clearly he, too, is disappointed for some reason.

"It was all a long time ago, wasn't it? And we were very young. You were quite right to go off and make your own way."

"No regrets?" It hurts to ask. It would have been better not to.

PETER tilts his dark head. I remember the softness of his hair sliding through my fingers and the brush of it against my cheek.

"No, we had to go our own separate ways, try our wings in the different directions that drew us at that time."

I'm sure he's right. I just wish he hadn't said it aloud.

"But they were good times, weren't they, Abi? D'you remember the afternoon we were out riding in the thunderstorm and we sheltered with the horses in the old quarry?"

"The crashing thunder and the horses whinnying —"

"And you said, 'Anyone who's never been kissed in a thunderstorm has never been kissed at all!' "

"I could never forget . . ." Peter's voice is hushed, thick with memories and the cobwebs of the past.

It's all flooding back now; the picnics, the climbs, the evenings spent walking hand-in-hand in the balmy air of that golden summer.

Peter hadn't been Mr Rich-and-Handsome, but for a few glorious months, he'd been mine.

"There hasn't been much time for picnicking since," Peter is saying. His voice cuts through my thoughts like a cold wind.

I feel suddenly sad to realise that he has probably put it all away in his mind the way one puts away childhood. But if he prefers to talk about the present, that's what we'll do.

I wave a hand around. "All this must be hard work."

"Very! It hasn't all been plain sailing, either. I've had employees who stocked their own kitchens at my expense, prima donna chefs and even a strike!"

"How awful!" If only I'd been here to help, I think absurdly.

We carry on talking but my mind is elsewhere.

Did he never miss me even occasionally, I wonder? Was all that effort and involvement with the business, that mixture of triumph and frustration, so absorbing that once I'd gone he never gave me a second thought?

I must be honest and realistic, though, why should he? It was me, after all, who chose to end the relationship. And I did have sound, sensible reasons, for doing so.

The tragedy is that none of them apply any more. Today we are not 20 and 18, we are adults.

Does my face betray me? I don't mean it to, but suddenly Peter is silent and reaches for my hand.

"We're two different people now," he says and I remember, with another sharp pang, how he could always read my thoughts. "But not quite strangers, because we have the past. Nothing can take that away."

I want to cry. He is being kind, he was always a kind person, but he obviously believes we can never have anything more than a shared past.

"You look sad, Abi."

I try to smile and shrug but I don't fool Peter.

His grip on my hand tightens. "Abi, perhaps you don't quite understand. Come outside, I want to show you something."

Puzzled, I slip off my stool and follow him between the solid, wooden tables.

He flicks a couple of switches just inside the main door and as we go out into the cool autumn night, the name of the café bursts into illumination above our heads.

Abigail's, it says.

"You thought I'd forgotten you, didn't you? While all these years I've been hoping you might, just might come back." And then I'm in his arms and it's as if the time between has only been hours.

"We have to get to know one another all over again, Abi."

"This is just a holiday," I protest faintly. "Don't forget I have my job . . ."

"We'll manage, Abi. We have to . . . Please say we can. I don't think I could bear to let you go again."

"Oh, Peter." That's all I can say. "Oh, Peter."

But deep down I feel as if I have come home. ∎

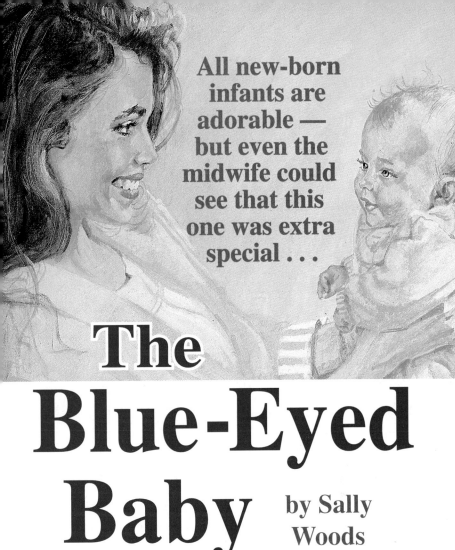

All new-born infants are adorable — but even the midwife could see that this one was extra special . . .

The
Blue-Eyed
Baby
by Sally Woods

A UDREY was convinced that in all her years as a midwife, she had never seen such a beautiful baby. This little girl had china-doll skin and eyes so big and blue they seemed to hypnotise.

She gazed down at the infant, lying in a crib alongside the hospital bed. The cherubic mouth was relaxed, yet one tiny fist was tightly clenched. When the little arm gave a sudden jerk, moving the blanket, Audrey immediately reached down to adjust the covers.

Her hand brushed against the child's. She gently stroked the delicate skin, marvelling at how perfectly formed the little hand was.

107

When the minute fist closed over her thumb, she experienced such a rush of tenderness that she had to swallow hard, scared that her emotions would give way to tears.

She allowed her hand to stay where it was, even after the big blue eyes had closed and the baby was asleep. Long lashes, the same colour as the down on her head, brushed the soft cheeks as she slept.

As Audrey watched the sleeping child, she began to imagine her as a toddler — mischievous perhaps, yet completely adorable. As a young girl — bewitchingly gorgeous but at the same time, very clever.

Somehow this baby looked very intelligent, even though she was only days old. Oh yes — she was bound to grow up with more than her fair share of genius!

Then, one day she would be a bride!

That image stayed with Audrey longer than the rest, for she could see in her mind a lovely young woman in a beautiful white dress.

The wedding veil covered her face, but underneath all that white lace, Audrey knew there would be such beauty that the man she was marrying would be the envy of dozens of disappointed suitors.

She smiled as she realised her imagination was running away with her.

Now she was just being silly! The baby was so young, yet here she was already, imagining her grown-up and married!

What would happen if she continually spent her time drooling over all the different children she helped to bring into the world? She would never get any work done!

A young nurse, who was new to the ward, came to stand behind Audrey. Peering over her shoulder into the cot she said, "What a beautiful baby!"

"Isn't she just!" Audrey replied.

"But then they all are," the nurse said with a smile, moving away.

Audrey continued to study the peacefully slumbering baby. She couldn't agree with that nurse! All right — she had to admit that, really, all babies were beautiful! But this one was more so.

Carefully withdrawing her thumb from the baby's hand so as not to wake her, Audrey wandered along the rest of the beds in the ward, chatting to the new mothers, asking how they were feeling.

Some were tired, some uncomfortable, but all of them somehow managed to radiate delight and happiness.

SHE peeked into the cribs beside the beds, too, admiring each new arrival as the proud mum smiled fondly.

Almost before she knew it, she had reached the ward doors.

"You must have delivered an awful lot of babies in your time," the young woman in the end bed remarked as Audrey approached. "Do you know how many — exactly?"

"I haven't a clue!" Audrey laughed. "It must be hundreds! Maybe more. I'm afraid I'm not one of those midwives who keeps count."

She turned and made her way back up the ward towards the blue-eyed baby.

Glancing down at her, Audrey told herself she had been right — this little mite definitely stood out from all the rest.

There wasn't another baby in the ward as beautiful as this one! In fact, she could safely say — in the whole wide world!

Yes, this one was special.

In a way the discovery was no great surprise. It merely confirmed what she had known all along.

The baby was still sleeping soundly. Audrey longed to reach down, lift her out of the cot, and hold her close. But it was much better to let her sleep.

She touched the small brow tenderly. "I hope you know I love you," she whispered. The baby didn't stir.

At that moment, a tall man with hair the same colour as the baby's came through the ward doors. "And how's my new daughter?" he asked, walking towards her, grinning broadly.

Audrey gazed up at her husband, and smiled. "Do you want my professional or my maternal opinion?" she asked with a grin.

"Both!" He smiled.

"Well . . . in that case, our daughter's wonderful — just wonderful." ■

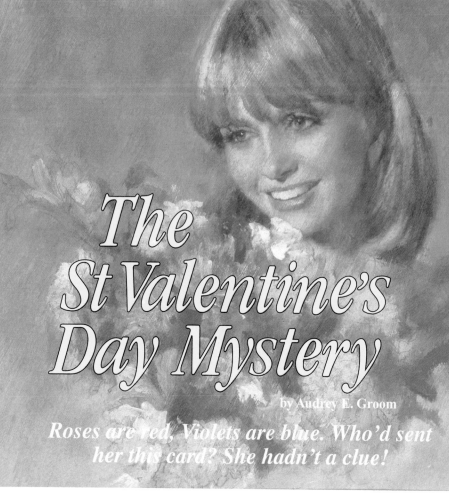

The St Valentine's Day Mystery

by Audrey E. Groom

Roses are red, Violets are blue. Who'd sent her this card? She hadn't a clue!

ATE as usual, I very nearly fell down the stairs only to see Mrs Carter, my landlady, sorting through the post in the hall. "Good morning," I called and rushed for the door — and would have been through it if she hadn't grabbed me back.

"Hey! Steady on there, Jenny. It's Valentine's Day! Surely you hadn't forgotten? There must be something here for you."

"Oh, what? No, no, I don't think so," I said, feeling the colour rising in my face.

"Oh, but there is. There you are!" She looked triumphant as she thrust a large, pink envelope into my hands.

"There you are, dear," she said again with a satisfied smile. "Miss J. Brown. No doubt about that, is there — or what it is? Didn't know he cared, did you?"

Didn't know he cared, I thought. Didn't know he existed, more like!

The grandfather clock in the hall struck 8.30, reminding me that I was really late now and hadn't time even to open the pink envelope.

"Thanks, anyway," I said, pushing it into my handbag. I could see she would have loved me to open it there and then.

But I'd only been in this job a couple of weeks and, already, I'd been late twice. So I knew I couldn't stop.

"I'll see you later," I said, giving her what I hoped was a special, compensating smile.

Then I dashed out and pelted down the road for the bus. It wasn't until I was swaying about on board it, packed in with the other sardines, that I even had time to think.

VALENTINE'S Day! Being an incurable romantic, I'd woven fantasies around it since I'd worn my first high heels. No, even before that, I suppose.

But I'd always been disappointed.

Even in my home-town in the West Country, I'd never had more than a couple of comic cards — except for that beautiful, romantic one last year — the one that my brother later admitted to sending, just for fun!

And, since I'd only been in London a short time and had, at most, made no more than a few acquaintances, who was there to even send me a funny card?

I decided not to open the envelope yet — after all, who'd want to open a comic Valentine in front of all these perfect strangers?

I preferred to wait till I was alone.

Struggling off the bus a while later, and on to the Tube, my thoughts were still with that unopened envelope, which, by this time, was practically burning a hole in my handbag.

However, when I finally made it to the office, I'd convinced myself it must be from an old school friend.

Or even my brother again — but I was still curious!

The office, bearing in mind what day it was, was even more of a hubbub of female chatter than usual.

In fact, they hardly seemed to notice me as I slipped between them to my desk in the corner, hearing bits of other people's conversations as I went.

"How many cards did you get?"

"Did Joe send you one?"

"Isn't this one romantic?"

"What a laugh! D'you know who sent that one?"

Obviously, Valentine's Day was the number one topic — and, incredibly, I found it was even getting to me. I'd intended to open mine later, when I was alone.

But surely, under cover of all this noise and excitement, they wouldn't even see me opening my "special delivery"?

I slipped it from my bag and out of its envelope.

I'd hardly had time to look at it before there were girls sitting on my desk and others peeping over my shoulder.

Someone grabbed the card from my hand.

"So, you got one, too, Jenny. You're a dark horse!"

"Let's see!"

"Let me see, too!"

"It's gorgeous, isn't it? D'you know who it's from?"

THE card eventually landed back on my desk and I was then able to see a picture of roses on the front.

Inside, under the printed message, Be My Valentine, were written the words, Because I think you're wonderful, in bold, red ink.

A lump came to my throat and, for a moment, I couldn't help feeling happy that someone had written such a message for me.

But, as I looked up, the spell was broken — any one of those girls, laughing and chatting noisily round my desk, could have sent it, just for fun.

The postmark was, after all, a London one.

Suddenly, though, everyone scattered — the office manager had just walked in and everybody did their best to look busy.

I logged on to my computer and, dropping the card back into my bag, I tried hard to forget it.

It wasn't easy, though, as a romantic aura quickly settled on the whole office.

By midday, a couple of desks had single red roses on them, several flowery-looking cards were propped up on in-trays and whispered phone conversations were getting longer and more numerous.

So were the faraway expressions.

Once or twice, when I was sure no-one was looking, I slipped my card out and looked at it again.

Of course it was a joke, I told myself — it couldn't be anything else. Or could it? Was it just possible that, out there, there was someone I didn't even know who fancied me?

It was unlikely, but it was also a nice, warm, romantic thought and I hugged it to myself all day.

THE Tube was less crowded than usual on the way home and a nice-looking man I saw quite often actually gave me a seat on the bus. Could he have sent the card, I wondered briefly?

But he got out at the next stop without another glance in my direction, and I told myself not to be so daft!

I decided on fish and chips for supper — not exactly romantic, but tasty.

When I returned to my digs, I was just about to dash up the stairs with my aromatic parcel, when Mrs Carter came into the hall.

She was carrying an enormous bunch of spring flowers.

"For you, Jenny," she said with a big, happy smile.

"For me!" I was so stunned I almost dropped the fish and chips.

I could only stare incredulously at her.

"Yes, for you, love," she repeated. "They came this afternoon. Look, there's a card tucked into them. See?"

I did see the card — and I could also see that she was almost as curious as I was to know what it said. So I hastily put the fish and chips down on the stairs and removed the card from its little envelope.

I still think you're wonderful, it read. I could hardly believe it. In fact, my hand shook a little as I turned the card for Mrs Carter to see the message, too.

Her round, motherly face broke out into a huge smile.

"Isn't that nice?" she enthused. "I think that's really smashing. He must think a lot of you, dear."

He? I thought. Who?

But all I said was, "Maybe, maybe, Mrs Carter," trying to sound mysterious but feeling my face going red.

"The flowers are lovely, anyway," I went on quickly. "And thanks a lot for taking them in.

"I must put them in water."

"Yes, of course," she said, as I picked up my supper again and rushed up to my room.

Carefully I filled the big, old vase that Mum had given me and arranged the flowers with loving care. There's something about daffodils, particularly, that remind me of sunshine and nice places — and nice people.

They especially made me think of spring days in Devon.

What did they remind him of, I wondered — the guy who had sent them? It had to be a man, didn't it? A genuine, sincere man, at that!

Surely no-one would send flowers just for fun? I took the Valentine card out of my bag and put it beside the flowers. Then, I stood admiring the effect of them together.

SUDDENLY, a knock on the door interrupted my thoughts. "Your landlady said it would be all right to come up," a male voice called out.

Curiously — and cautiously — I opened my door to see who was there.

The man standing there was tall and slim, with one of those rather ordinary, yet interesting, faces that come to life with a smile. Only the smile on his face faded when he saw me and changed to a frown.

"A girl I — er — know — used to live —" he began.

"She left here a few weeks ago," I quickly told him.

"Her surname was Brown."

"So's mine," I replied, my heart sinking. How could I have forgotten that

113

fact so completely — until now. Mrs Carter had mentioned the coincidence when I moved in. But after that she'd simply referred to her as Irene.

I didn't have to say any more — neither did he.

I watched the happy anticipation disappear from his eyes and instinctively knew that the disappointment that was beginning to cloud his face must be showing on mine, too.

"I'm awfully sorry," he said.

"I'm sorry, too," I replied.

But, even as I said that, I couldn't quite think what I was sorry for — except for being the wrong girl!

And I couldn't help that!

He looked around awkwardly, not knowing what else to say now. He obviously didn't wish to rush off, and yet he had no reason to stay now.

He turned vaguely towards the stairs.

"The flowers," I called out suddenly. "Would you like the flowers back?"

"What? Oh, no!" He looked horrified. "Please, keep them — really, I'd rather you kept them."

Our eyes met then and I knew he was unhappy and possibly as lonely as I was.

Perhaps that's what prompted me to ask, "Would you — would you like a cup of coffee?"

Instantly his face lit up again in a warm smile. He hesitated for only a second, then he said, "Yes, I would — if you're sure you don't mind."

"I don't mind at all."

He followed me in, stopping by the flowers and looking down at where the card lay open on the table. "I really am sorry," he said again sincerely.

I shrugged and smiled. "Not to worry. That's Valentine's Day for you, isn't it?"

When I brought the coffee, he told me his name was Paul.

"Pleased to meet you, Paul," I said. "And I'm Jenny."

"I think I should explain . . ." he began.

"It would be interesting."

"You see, I work in the local library. And there was this girl . . . she used to come in quite often. I longed to talk to her, but I hadn't the courage.

"I'm a bit shy I suppose, where girls are concerned. But I discovered her name and address from her library ticket."

"Ah, yes — my namesake, Miss Brown."

"Yes. Miss I. Brown."

"Oh dear. My name's Jenny — I couldn't have noticed the initial was an 'I' and not a 'J'."

"Well, anyway," he continued, "I thought perhaps Valentine's Day was a good time to break the ice. And that, once I'd sent the card and the flowers, I could drop by myself.

"Only it's all too late now."

He sipped his coffee thoughtfully and I nodded understandingly.

"Of course," he said after a few moments, "I'd probably have been too tongue-tied to speak to her properly anyway.

"She seemed very intellectual, taking out books on sociology and psychology and spending ages in the reference library."

I couldn't help laughing ruefully. "I'm into Catherine Cookson myself."

"And I'm really a Frederick Forsyth and Tom Clancy man." We laughed together.

"Wait a minute," I said, suddenly inspired. "Do you like fish and chips, too?

"Could you eat half a portion, if I heat them up in the microwave?"

"What an offer!" he declared. "How could I refuse? Shall I nip out and pick up a bottle of wine to go with it?"

WHEN he returned, we tucked into fish and chips, hunks of bread and cheese, bananas and a bottle of wine.

It was a wonderful meal and, by the time we'd finished it, we'd discussed everything from books to old buildings, politics to sport, films to television.

And we had remarkably similar taste in all of them! Even a similar sense of humour to cap it all!

"It's funny, isn't it?" Paul said suddenly. "But I don't feel tongue-tied or shy with you at all."

I couldn't stop the blush rising to my cheeks.

"Could you face another evening with me, Jenny?" Paul asked as he was leaving. "The theatre, or a film perhaps — you choose."

"I'd like that," I replied. "A film would be nice."

"I'll pick you up on Saturday, then, about seven. Is that OK?"

"That'll be fine," I said. "Thank you, Paul. Thanks for everything."

He put out his hand and took mine for a moment. "Thank you, Miss Jenny Brown," he said formally, before breaking into a huge, warm smile that I automatically returned.

When he'd gone, I crossed to the table and stood looking down at the beautiful daffodils again — and was intrigued to see the card now had extra writing on it.

My heart hammering, I picked it up.

Beneath the Be My Valentine it read, Because I think you're wonderful, Jenny. With love from Paul.

How sweet of him to have done that! That way, he made the flowers and the card really mine.

What a fantastic, truly romantic Valentine's Day it had turned out to be after all. And I couldn't help thinking it could well be the first of many. ■

Chase The White Horses

by Susan Lane

The promise was
one she knew
could not
be kept —
but she
didn't reckon
on the power
of love . . .

THE sun-lounge of the small hotel overlooked the beach. Only fine ribbons of rain interrupted the view of the deserted shoreline, and the sand at the water's edge was smooth and shiny.

Further out the afternoon sky seemed almost to drop down to touch the sea, hiding the horizon behind a silver mist.

"It's a sea-fret," Richard said. He sat facing the window, looking small and pale in the large armchair. A bright woollen blanket lay across his knees, for the east coast air was surprisingly chill and damp for August, and Richard, with his asthma, was a delicate child.

Rachel glanced up from her book and noticed that, once again, her son's gaze was remote and shadowed.

"Never mind," she said, too brightly to sound convincing. "The donkeys will be back tomorrow."

Richard nodded gravely. He had spent most of the holiday helping out with the donkeys on the beach.

He loved their sweet natures and velvety muzzles, but they couldn't make up for not having seen the white horses that Daddy had promised he would

117

see — beautiful white horses, glittering and galloping over the waves.

He wouldn't mention them to his mother, though. Not again. When they had first arrived here, he'd asked her about the white horses.

She'd gone very quiet, and her eyes had looked unhappy. Then she'd pointed to the breeze-curled waves with their white foamy edges.

"Those are the white horses, Richard." Her voice had been gentle but firm, and for some reason Richard had felt unable to tell her that he needed to believe in the horses his father had described so vividly.

Daddy had promised he would see them — the way he'd also promised that he would always love Richard, and be there for him. Now he stared silently out to sea and wondered how he could believe in one promise without the other.

One white horse would do, he thought sadly. Just one white, galloping horse would make everything all right again . . .

THE next day dawned bright and fair. A mild breeze dotted the sea with tiny white crests.

"A perfect day." Rachel smiled, as they trudged through soft, gritty sand towards the donkeys.

Richard stroked their gentle, questing noses, and Joe the donkey-man beamed, his red, wind-scoured face breaking into a web of friendly wrinkles.

"Free rides today for my helper of the week!" he declared, lifting Richard effortlessly into the saddle of a tall, black donkey. "How old did you say you were?" he asked cheerfully.

"Seven." Richard carefully gathered up his reins. Joe nodded, pretending to be deep in thought, and winked reassuringly at Rachel. She smiled back, genuinely liking the old man.

"Seven." Joe grinned. "Old enough to take Pedro along to the rock, then, I think."

"By myself?" Richard looked both startled and pleased. He squeezed his heels into Pedro's soft sides and the donkey ambled off. Rachel watched anxiously, then turned, sensing Joe's eyes upon her.

"It's good to see the lad smile," he remarked quietly. "He's keen on the donkeys."

"And horses." Rachel sighed softly, her mind drifting back to their first morning here, and Richard's questions.

"His father told him he would see white horses, galloping in from the sea. He's been so disappointed to find they're only waves. I can't console him."

"Ah." Joe cast her a shrewd glance. "He's never mentioned his father," he said slowly.

"No." Rachel looked away. "Christopher — my husband — died six months ago." She hesitated. Suddenly, words she'd needed to say for so long, but never had, began to tumble out. "Christopher was a marvellous father — he made everything somehow magical. Even when he was ill, he had a way of making dreams come true for Richard — in the way that I can't." She lowered her head in despair, feeling a familiar tingle of anger and sadness rise within her.

"Now Richard stares out to sea with that disappointed expression when he thinks I'm not looking — and I can't help him." Her eyes filled with tears.

"But you just have." Joe's sun-faded eyes twinkled. "White horses aren't an impossibility, you know."

"No?" Rachel asked, puzzled.

"Certainly not!" Joe shook his head insistently.

Rachel smiled hopefully and sat down upon the soft sand to listen.

Late that night, Rachel and Richard waited in the sun-lounge of the hotel. Richard stared out over the dark beach.

"Tonight, Mummy?" His voice was awed and hushed. "Did the donkey-man say the white horses would come tonight?"

"Yes. It was definitely tonight." Rachel crossed her fingers. Joe had promised and she trusted him, but if something should go wrong . . .

She glanced at the clock. It was almost midnight.

L ISTEN!" Richard sat forward suddenly. Rachel strained her ears until, far off, amidst the low boom of the surf, she heard a faint rhythmic pounding.

"There!" Richard pressed his face to the window. The grey mare appeared out of the darkness, just as Joe had promised she would. Rachel smiled.

It was true that the mare wasn't actually one of the slender, ethereal creatures Christopher had talked of — she was stocky and heavy-legged.

But as she cantered freely along the water's edge, she was beautiful enough to chase the unhappiness from Richard's face.

He watched intently until the mare had cantered out of sight and then Rachel felt his hand squeeze hers.

"Look, Mummy!" he whispered excitedly. "Look at the sea!"

Rachel looked — and blinked. Afterwards, she would tell herself that they'd stared too hard at the mare; that the pale image had lingered and somehow multiplied against the dark background of the sea.

Because, for a few timeless seconds, it seemed that graceful white horses danced on the waves.

Tossing manes, flying tails and striking hooves glittered out amongst the curling foam, and then they faded, leaving only the darkness — and a sudden, sure sense of love all around them. Christopher's love.

Richard turned to her. "Daddy promised," he whispered. "But you made it happen, Mummy — because you believed."

For a moment, the air was hushed. Even the sea seemed to hold its breath as Rachel saw the joy in Richard's eyes, and she knew that the love and beauty of this magical summer night had chased all the shadows away forever. ■

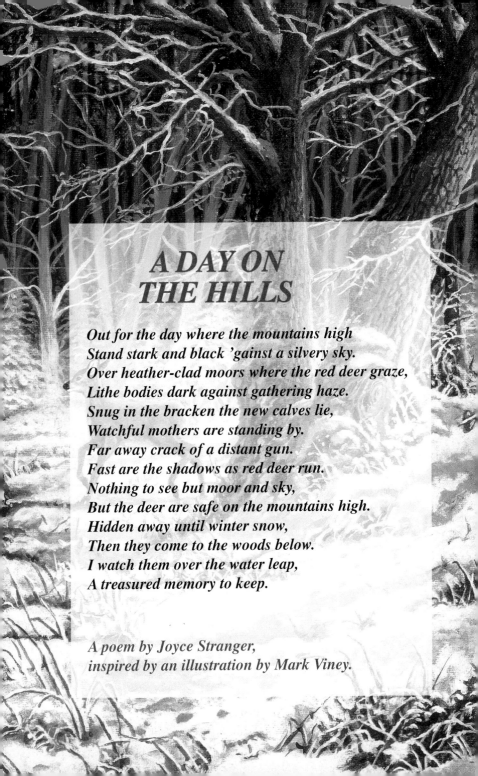

A DAY ON THE HILLS

Out for the day where the mountains high
Stand stark and black 'gainst a silvery sky.
Over heather-clad moors where the red deer graze,
Lithe bodies dark against gathering haze.
Snug in the bracken the new calves lie,
Watchful mothers are standing by.
Far away crack of a distant gun.
Fast are the shadows as red deer run.
Nothing to see but moor and sky,
But the deer are safe on the mountains high.
Hidden away until winter snow,
Then they come to the woods below.
I watch them over the water leap,
A treasured memory to keep.

A poem by Joyce Stranger,
inspired by an illustration by Mark Viney.

Last Summer Of Childhood

by Jean Davis

The lessons I learned
then were difficult —
but they held good
for ever . . .

122

I ALWAYS thought Great-Aunt Julia was ancient, and reckoned that she went back in time, if not to Victoria, then at least to the elegance and languor of the Edwardian era.

In fact, she had grown up in the 1920s, had served in the Wrens during the War and was a high-powered Civil Servant before retiring to a relaxed, pleasant life in what had once been a fisherman's cottage on the Norfolk coast.

We spent part of our summer holidays there each year, though not actually in her cottage — Mother said she wouldn't inflict Dick and me upon Aunt Julia's sheltered life.

We stayed in the bungalow next door. It was practical and slightly drab, decorated in greens, dirty yellows and browns, except for the sitting-room, which must have been the legacy of a moment of madness suffered by a previous owner.

Three walls were papered in maroon and saffron regency stripes, while the forth sported scarlet and puce cabbage roses.

I was sure that there were purple humming-birds in among the flora, but Dick said I needed to have my eyes tested.

Dick was a distant cousin of mine. He spent all his holidays with us, because his parents were working abroad, in the Gold Coast.

"You'd see fairies at the bottom of the garden, you would," he scoffed, and I yelled back that he was mean and horrid, that there was nothing wrong with my eyes, and that he was the one who couldn't see things for looking at them.

He ignored this clever repartee, and I went out in a sulk on to the sand dunes, because I knew that there were fairies at the bottom of some gardens.

GREAT-AUNT JULIA and my mother were very fond of each other. They used to tease one another all the time, saying things that made my head jerk up in alarm. But they never argued — they just smiled affectionately, and laughed.

I would breathe a sigh of relief, because life had a nasty habit of producing moments of terror, when grown-ups stopped being infallible and wise, and were, suddenly, at loggerheads.

Then the firm ground that was my immutably safe and self-centred world shifted like the sand I plodded through to reach the firm, wet edge of the sea.

That was the year when there were sudden silences as Dick and I burst in through the open front door, when Mother and Great-Aunt stopped talking, cut off in mid-sentence.

"You'll have to make up your mind, one way or the other —"

Aunt Julia's voice was both angry and sad.

"How long are you going to let it go on?"

And once it was Mother, small, plump, quiet and gentle Mother, saying, "I'd kill her, if I could get near her. I never knew what hate meant until now."

"Then fight . . ."

"Fight? Me?"

Dick didn't seem to notice the tension in the atmosphere, but I looked from Julia to my mother in a mixture of fear and dread. Dick grew impatient with the silence and pushed me out of the way, hurting my arm so that I cried out.

Great-Aunt Julia intervened then, putting a comforting arm around my shoulders. I was crying, and not just because of my arm, but Dick didn't understand.

I knew that it was all because Dad wasn't with us. This was the first time he hadn't come, and nobody mentioned him, or gave us any reasons or excuses.

I thought that was odd, because he and Great-Aunt Julia had always been such friends.

They usually took us out during the day, leaving Mother to potter around the house or sit, reading, in the conservatory, while the wind swept across the sea — all the way from Siberia, Dad said.

They let us paddle and watch the grey tide lapping on to the shore, giving us time to watch the changing colours as our footprints were swallowed up in the shallow water.

MY dad was a chef, and he worked in a big hotel in the town where we lived.

He was not like other girls' fathers, off for the early train, and home again for tea in the evening.

Sometimes he left at six, to do breakfasts and lunches; sometimes he had to go in from mid-afternoon until midnight, or later.

Mother would tell me sometimes that there was a function on, and I would sigh, because that meant he wouldn't come home until I was asleep, and in the morning, I'd have to be quiet, so that he could have a lie-in.

But recently, Mother hadn't mentioned functions, and Dad hadn't been home very often. When I trudged home from school, heavy with books and sports gear, I was met with silence.

There were no calls of, "How's my girl, then?" or, "It can't be that time, surely?" from Dad.

And when I tip-toed around first thing in the morning, Mother would say, tight-lipped, "It's all right, your dad isn't asleep. He decided to stay at the hotel, because he would be so late. He didn't want to disturb us."

Eventually, he hardly came home at all, except to collect clean underwear, shirts and the white overalls and chef's hats which Mother laundered with such care.

When we were on holiday, Dick would often go clambering on the rocks on the shore below the enormous church.

It had been built in the days when the sea came right up to the line of what was now the road, when the village had been a thriving port.

Each Sunday, when Mother insisted that we accompanied her to the service, I thought how lonely the small congregation looked, lost among the soaring arches and tattered flags. One day, when Dick was out with a friend, Great-Aunt Julia and I tramped down to the shore.

She strode slightly ahead of me, her bare feet scarlet-toed and her mop of grey curls blowing unchecked in the breeze.

"Who does Mother hate?" I blurted out suddenly.

I'd been waiting for this moment to ask her, when there were just the two of us, beneath the high, cloud-scudding sky.

"Hate? Your mother doesn't know how to hate," she began.

"But she said . . ."

She looked sideways at me, the grey eyes keen.

"Well, I suppose you're old enough. How old are you now?"

"Eleven, nearly twelve —"

"How time flies," she muttered. "Well, how many times have you been told about getting into bad company? That somebody isn't a fit companion for you to be friends with?"

"Not many, but a few. Mother says it to Dick quite often. For a start, she doesn't like that Fatty Bolam he's out with today."

"Well, your dad has got in with some people your mother doesn't approve of. Particularly this one woman who works at the hotel —"

"You mean Mrs O'Leary? Oh, I know her."

SHE'D come with Dad once, when he'd taken me and Dick to the zoo. On that stifling hot day, the animals had panted on the shadeless concrete, and I'd been sick.

She'd blamed the ice-cream and the doughnut I'd eaten, calling me "Greedy". That had been unfair — Dick had eaten twice as much as me.

But no-one else seemed to feel the utter dispiritedness and despair of those poor, imprisoned animals, and nobody seemed to understand why I was heart-sick.

Then there had been the local funfair. Mother didn't like crowds and noise, so she'd asked Dad to take us.

He'd brought along Mrs O'Leary, in her high heels and with her blonde beehive hair-do setting off the pink and white china of her face.

She'd squealed with terror on the dodgems, when Dick and I rammed into them.

The big wheel had made her "feel all faint", so that she'd clutched on to Dad, and she'd hung on to his arm when he was shooting, making him miss.

He'd shrugged, laughing, and said, "You can't win 'em all!"

I thought of all that as Great-Aunt Julia said, "If only your mother would go out and meet life, instead of letting it go by."

I jumped to her defence. "She just likes being quiet. Mother hates noise and lots of people and quarrelling —" I broke off lamely.

We sat down on the coarse grass, and looked out across the restless sea.

"Have you ever wondered why I'm not married?" she asked.

I blushed, embarrassed at such a grown-up question.

"I was engaged, towards the end of the war." She spoke into the wind, deliberately not looking at me.

"He was in the navy, and I was the typical sophisticated society girl, the life and soul of our crowd.

"We were very much in love, but then I realised he was very interested — too interested — in another girl, so different from me. She was quiet and mousy — yielding and peaceful."

She could have been talking about my mother, but, with the ruthless logic of youth, I worked out the age difference, and watched her brown-flecked hands, as she pulled up a blade of grass and tore it into pieces.

"I fought for his love. Oh, how I fought! And I won. He went back to sea, and I had triumphed, I was wearing his ring. It was me he cared for, not Amy. Or so I thought."

There was a long silence, broken only by the wind, and the sad cries of the gulls.

"What happened?" I asked timidly. "Why didn't you marry?"

"And live happily ever after? Oh, life does things to you — circumstances change. I'd always wanted to go overseas, and suddenly, I was posted abroad.

"I came home when the war ended to find that he hadn't waited, and there they were, married, with a bouncy baby son —"

I WAS lost. Grown-ups didn't bare their souls to children, not then, not in our family. Grown-ups knew it all. They were judge and jury, comforters and stout upholders of the laws that they made.

I still didn't quite know why she was telling me all this. Dimly I realised she was asking me to encourage my mother to fight, to turn her into someone she could never be, and so I said, "But there's nothing we can do, is there?"

"I've already done it." She stood up, digging her feet into the shifting sand.

"I've written to your father, telling him to pull himself together, and be grateful for what he has, not to go dancing after rainbows and false promises. Not when he's got your mother."

I stood, too, my fine mousy hair blowing over my face.

"I shouldn't have burdened you with all this," she said, "but I had to talk to somebody. Let's go back."

There was a motorbike outside the bungalow when we got there — Dad's old Norton. I ran inside, calling, "Dad, Dad, is it really you?" and he let go Mother's hand, rising from the settee to catch me in his arms.

"How's my girl, then? My, how you've grown since you've been here. It must be the sea air."

He looked over my head at Julia as I wriggled away, not ready yet to forgive and forget, and I caught the exchange of glances between them.

GREAT-AUNT JULIA left everything she had to Dick and me when she died, in trust for our son. We returned to the village after so many years away, and we laughed together at the tender ghosts, and walked, full of memories, along the shore.

Of course, things had changed — the beach was tamed, and there were new hotels and roads. The fishermen's cottages had picture windows and garages, and brightly-painted front doors.

I told Dick about that talk I'd had with Great-Aunt Julia all those years ago, as we, in our turn, sat on the sand dunes, looking out over that same but ever-changing sea.

"I remember that holiday," he said slowly. "It was the first time, I think, that I started to see you all — but you particularly — as people, and not just as part of my comfort."

I laughed. "You were pretty arrogant as a boy. But then, I suppose that's part of a happy childhood — to think that everyone else is just there for your own convenience."

We sat in the companionable silence of those who share friendship as well as love, and I said, "Great-Aunt watched over us all that summer. Dad never really settled, and I seemed to spend a lot of time telling Mother to fight and be more positive."

"You always were a fighter." He grinned at me. "Remember how we used to fight, all the time?"

"That was different, fighting *with* somebody — it was fighting *for* someone that Julia meant. But Mother never let the hurt show — she was always loyal.

"She used to tell me not to worry so much. She said that Dad would always come back, because after a while he got tired of the excitement, and the complications."

Dick took my hand, and said easily, "Ah, well, it's all over now. The past is dead, with them. Nothing can be changed now."

We strolled back to finish sorting out the papers and the furniture in the cottage, and already the imprint of Great-Aunt Julia was fading.

For all her fighting, I reflected, she'd lost her heart's desire, while my mother had kept her love intact, refusing to let her faith be shattered.

I wondered then, as I had wondered many times over the years, who had been right; and often, too, I'd wondered how differently things would have been if my grandmother had been Julia, and not Amy . . . ■

Worlds Apart

by Hermione Peters

Even then, in that time of great uncertainty, he was sure she was the girl for him . . .

THE greying military moustache almost accentuates the sensitivity in the features of the face. His appearance is neat but not loud. The raincoat which covers his dark blue suit is from a good outfitter.

Without being ostentatious, nothing about him looks cheap, though he himself looks uneasy in the theatre foyer.

He is unaccompanied and stands looking about him as though not quite certain what to do or where to go next, as though in fact his visits to the theatre were too infrequent for him to feel in place in one.

He slips his hand into his coat pocket, looks down in surprise, and produces from the pocket a black leather glove. Surprise is replaced by sudden delight and he smiles at some private recollection, for a moment oblivious to all around him.

Once he had found a similar glove in the pocket of another coat. That coat had been part of his Naval uniform.

Ah! What an awkward, tongue-tied young man he had been in those days! And how terrified he had been in case he should betray his small-town Canadian breeding among the English ladies to whom he'd been introduced.

The ladies' committee of the local gentry had arranged a special ball to welcome the Canadians to their country.

It was an exciting event for a young serviceman like him who'd only ever been able to imagine such traditional, English, upper-class events.

ON his return to the mess, he had found that other glove. And he had danced not once, not twice, but three times with the auburn-haired young woman who must have put it there.

She had indeed captivated him and he had wondered whether it would be considered proper or even wise to fall in love with her before he realised he had already fallen.

The people she was with had given him a lift back to the base in their car and he had shared the back seat with her.

That, no doubt, was when she had slipped the glove into his pocket. It was like her, the glove, petite and neat. Quality.

He had lived long enough to recognise it, in people as well as in things. Especially in people.

When they had been dancing together, he had said to her the things he thought he ought to. He had read these words, even then fascinated by things

129

British, in the romantic English novels his mother used to buy, and which he'd read after her as a boy.

"Do you enjoy dancing?" "Do you often go dancing?" "The band's good, isn't it!" He hadn't put a foot wrong. And now?

It was plain as Punch the glove was a sign, a signal, a message. That was the sort of thing people in love did to show the other how they felt.

It was a love token. He'd known she felt something for him, known it, felt it. And it was confirmed. The glove confirmed it. It was . . . a declaration! He had to respond, and as soon as possible.

HE woke late the Sunday morning after the ball, and realised immediately that something wonderful had happened the night before.

Of course! He had fallen in love.

He was in love and his love was returned. But in love with whom? To his consternation he found that he did not even know her name.

After breakfast he joined a group of guys from his unit discussing the ball and casually asked one of the men, "There was a an auburn-haired, English girl I danced with. Did you see us?"

"I think so."

"D'you know who she was?"

"Aha!" interjected another, and rolled his eyes meaningfully round the group.

"I just wondered," he put in, trying to camouflage his interest.

"He means Irene Rolandson," the first one told the group. Then turning to him, he added, "She's not really right for you, pal. She's 'county,' up-town — out of your league."

THERE were not nearly so many names in the telephone directory in those days, and there were only two Rolandsons. He dialled the first of these, and as luck would have it, Irene herself answered the phone.

"Irene! This is Robert Carey. We danced together last night. You remember? The Canadian sailor."

"I remember very well."

She remembered very well! Excellent!

"When can we meet?"

A pause. He feared she would hear the beating of his heart over the line, it seemed so loud.

"How soon do you want to meet?"

"Very soon!"

Another pause. "Can you get over to the Ram's Head at Littlemoor this afternoon?"

"Of course!" he said delightedly.

"I pass it with the dogs when I take them for a walk. I'll be there about three o'clock."

There was a click as she put down the receiver.

He'd made it. His first date with Irene. There would, he knew, be many more. He didn't care that they were from different countries, different backgrounds.

Quick, find a bus timetable. Yes, there is a bus, even on a Sunday. It leaves in half an hour and there isn't another till late in the afternoon.

He'd have four hours or so to kill before he met Irene and he'd miss a meal-break. He might even have to walk the 12 miles home, but somehow none of those things mattered in the slightest.

On a table in the mess-hall stood a vase of roses. In those days it was unusual to find flowers out of season, but behind the mess were some greenhouses and the mess sergeant was a rose fancier. Much to the amusement of the men he often arranged a vase or two.

One of these roses, a lush dark red one, the young sailor took from the vase and placed with the glove, darting into the dining-room to steal a napkin in which to wrap the two.

Then he put on his hat and greatcoat and made for the entrance.

WHEN Irene appeared in the distance with two lumbering Labradors, he forgot how cold his feet were, how stiff his limbs were from waiting, and went joyfully towards her, turning over in his mind the words he should greet her with. But she was the first to speak.

"Hello there. There was such urgency in your voice when you rang, I thought this was the best time to meet."

Her manner was kind and not unfriendly, but cooler than he had anticipated, so that he was a little taken aback.

"Oh, er, how are you?" he asked, feeling a little let down.

"I'm very well indeed, thank you."

"Did you enjoy last night?"

She laughed in evident surprise. "Yes, it was great fun."

"I enjoyed it, too."

"Do stop talking like someone in a tuppenny novelette and tell me why you wanted to see me so urgently."

Now it was his turn to be surprised and a little uneasy.

"Because of this!" And he proffered the little packet of the glove and the rose wrapped in the serviette, this last now crumpled and damp.

"It's a rose!"

"No, the glove!"

"Whose is it?"

He felt suddenly faint with fear and mortification. "Why, it's yours, isn't it?"

She looked at him intently for a moment, then replied, "It isn't my glove. Where did it come from?"

"I found it in my greatcoat pocket last night, after the ride with you in the car . . ."

"How did you get here today?" she asked suddenly, a small frown creasing her forehead.

"I came here by bus . . ." he answered.

"There hasn't been a bus for hours. You must have been waiting . . .!"

She burst into laughter, covering her mouth with her hand. The gesture was so child-like, it made him smile. "Someone must have picked up the glove in the cloakroom and stuffed it into the wrong pocket."

They both began to speak at once, and he forgot all about what was proper to say and what was not.

They chatted easily and naturally together and were soon deep in conversation as though they'd known each other for years.

"You must be frozen," she said at last. "Come home and have some tea and meet Mummy and Daddy."

★ ★ ★ ★

The old gentleman in the theatre foyer chuckles.

"What are you smiling about?" A woman of his own age appears at his side.

"I found this in my pocket," he says with a smile.

"I've been looking everywhere for the wretched thing. I had to wear a pair which don't match my bag," she tells him with a sigh.

He bends towards her and whispers.

"There ought to be a rose . . ."

The woman looks at him quizzically for a second, then smiles tenderly up at him, realising the significance of his words.

There are still strands of fine auburn hair among the grey on her head . . . ■

LUCY'S LOST

by Elizabeth Farrant

Could a missing cat come between two sisters — or bring them closer together?

MARY JOHNSON opened the kitchen door and peered out anxiously across her small back garden. But, just as she'd feared, there was still no sign of Lucy.

It was almost dark — and, to make matters worse, it had begun to rain. A cold, grey drizzle, ready to turn itself into a downpour at any minute.

Mary couldn't understand it. Lucy had always had the usual cat's dislike of rainy weather — and so she seldom stayed out late.

But tonight — Mary had to face it — tonight was different. Lucy was not just late — Lucy was missing. And she'd been missing now for two whole days . . .

133

Lucy was quite an ordinary cat — no pedigree, no great beauty. Black and white, with white across her nose which made her small, pert face look rather like a clown's. But she was Mary's cat — they understood each other, she and Lucy.

Hot tears pricked Mary's eyes at the sight of the old blue saucer on the mat. Already it seemed so meaningless, somehow. Would Lucy ever lap from it again, she wondered — her rough pink tongue scouring it clean as new?

Only two days ago she'd taken Lucy's quiet routine for granted. But now she'd have given anything for a glimpse of that small, clown-like face peeping around the door.

It was no use — she'd have to search again. Just once, she thought, before it got really dark . . .

She reached for her old grey cardigan and pulled it round her shoulders. Her slippers squelched on the cold, wet grass, as she wandered up and down the tiny square of lawn, calling out softly, urgently, "Here, Lucy . . . Lucy . . . Lucy . . ."

"Mary! Mary! Come in, for goodness' sake, before you catch your death of cold!"

The voice from the kitchen window startled her and, for one brief moment, anxiety gave place to irritation.

Flo had been watching her — she might have known it.

It was just three weeks since Flo, her older sister, had sold up her home and come to live with Mary. Three weeks of strain, bickering and discomfort. To Mary they'd seemed more like years.

Yet it had seemed a good idea at first. Since her husband, Angus, had died two years before, Mary had been quite alone except, of course, for Lucy.

"Best thing for both of you," her friends had said. "It doesn't make sense — two sisters living alone in two separate houses. And let's face it — neither of you is getting any younger . . ."

"It's such a relief," her married daughter told her, "knowing you'll have Aunt Flo for company."

All that made sense, of course, Mary told herself. But even so she'd felt a tiny niggle of uneasiness. She remembered so well what Angus used to say — two females in one kitchen — that's bound to spell trouble . . .

And Angus had been so right — she knew that now. Till she and Flo had set up house together, she'd forgotten just how bossy Flo could be . . .

NOW, as Mary slowly pushed the back door open, she found her sister busy at the sink, tut-tutting over the fact that Mary had left the washing-up half-done to go and look for her cat.

"I'm surprised at you, Mary Johnson. Where do you keep your tea-towels? This one's soaking wet. And these kitchen drawers are in a right old muddle. No wonder I can never lay my hands on anything . . ."

Pausing when she saw the hurt look on Mary's face, her voice was a little softer as she added, "Cheer up, now, Mary. That cat'll be back, you'll see. All cats go wandering every now and then — it's in their nature."

Mary shook her head. "Not my Lucy."

Lucy, she thought, had always been a little like herself. Real homebirds, both of them . . .

But then, she reminded herself, home in these past three weeks had been so different — for Lucy as well as herself. Flo had shown no concern for Lucy's feelings.

On more than one occasion she'd shooed her off her favourite fireside chair and had laughed scornfully when Mary had timidly spoken up for her pet.

No, nothing had been the same since Flo moved in. If it hadn't been for Flo, Mary told herself, Lucy might still be here . . .

"If you ask me, Mary," Flo's voice broke into her thoughts, "I think it's a change you need. Something to take you out of yourself, I mean. It's bingo evening at the over-sixties club. How about us going along, just for an hour or so?"

"Oh, no. No thanks, I couldn't. Not tonight."

Flo just didn't understand, Mary told herself. At a time like this, how could she hope to concentrate on bingo? And besides, she'd never forgive herself if Lucy came back and there was no-one in.

"You go, though," she added. "I mean, it's not as if . . ."

She broke off as the evening paper dropped through the letter-box and landed on the mat. Grabbing it eagerly, she rummaged in her handbag for her spectacles. Of course, she thought, the Lost and Found column . . .

"Flo — listen to this!" she gasped a moment later.

But Flo was upstairs, changing her dress, preparing for her bingo.

MARY read the notice for a second time. It was the first of the items in the column. Talk about luck, she thought . . .

Tears blurred the small print — tears of relief this time. Found — black female cat, white markings . . . And there was a number to phone.

Of course it was Lucy. It just had to be her Lucy . . .

Mary slipped on her outdoor clothes with unaccustomed haste, taking her stout brown shopping-basket from the cupboard underneath the stairs.

Lucy had travelled in it more than once, on occasions when she'd visited the vet.

Tonight it would be a much happier journey. Lucy was coming home.

When Flo came bustling down, Mary was ready and pulling on her woollen gloves. "Now, Mary if you're going out, mind you put your scarf on. And your hat, too!"

Trust Flo, Mary thought. Fussing and interfering as usual.

"There's a cold wind tonight," Flo continued, "and you know how weak your chest is. We don't want you laid up, do we?"

In a daze, Mary accepted the woolly scarf Flo offered and hurried off towards the nearest phone-box. Now that she'd come so close to finding Lucy, Flo's sharp tongue didn't bother her so much.

Flo meant well, after all. It was just that she, Mary, had always been the "little sister" — and Flo would always think of her that way.

Mary's mind went drifting back to early childhood when she'd always run to Flo with all her small disasters. Anything from a lost hair-ribbon to a blotted exercise book had made her seek comfort in Flo's arms.

Strong, safe, reliable Flo had replaced the mother Mary had never known.

Mary smiled to herself as those early memories came crowding back. She'd tried Flo's patience often enough in those days. The voice of a younger Flo came back across the years . . .

"Oh, dear — you'll be the death of me, our Mary . . ."

But Flo had always been good company. They'd had some laughs together in the old days . . .

Her thoughts were jerked back swiftly to the present by the sight of a phone-box just a few yards away. Mary crept in cautiously. She'd always hated public telephones.

Peering suspiciously at the instructions, she rummaged in her purse for the required 10p and carefully dialled the number.

A woman's voice answered. It sounded young and friendly.

"Hello? Oh, yes — it was me who put the advertisement in the paper. Yes . . . yes — the cat's still here . . ."

The house, it turned out, was not so far away. Ten minutes later Mary was standing in the open doorway, anticipation shining in her eyes.

But seconds afterwards she was staring across the hall, swallowing her disappointment — for the cat which came to meet her wasn't Lucy.

"I'm sorry," she said, her voice trembling, "but it isn't mine . . ." She brushed away a tear.

"I'm sorry, too." The girl — she wasn't much more than a girl, after all,

Mary thought — glanced from the cat to Mary and hesitated.

"I was just thinking . . . if you've lost your own cat . . . well, I took this one in," the girl went on, softly, "because she was hungry, and it was obvious she was a stray.

"But Don — my husband — is allergic to cats . . . and so I can't really keep this one much longer . . ."

The cat, oblivious to this revelation, began to purr softly and rub itself around Mary's ankles. Mary felt a sudden little stab of pity. The cat was not much more than a kitten, full of life, she thought — just like her Lucy.

She sighed and hesitated, then sighed again. "I'll take her," she muttered finally.

Then, scarcely aware of the girl's relief and her smiles of gratitude, Mary walked out slowly through the lighted hall into the cold dark night.

By now it was raining hard, and the weight of the basket clutched against her chest was as heavy as her heart.

She arrived home cold and damp and miserable. And tired — too tired to think. Almost too tired to feel the loss of Lucy.

Easing herself into her rocking-chair she sat for a little while, her eyes half-closed, while the strange cat explored its new surroundings, approved them and curled up neatly on the hearth-rug.

Mary was relieved that Flo had gone to bingo. There'd be time enough for tiresome explanations later.

Meanwhile she'd put the kettle on, she thought. She could do with a cup of tea.

THE moment she stirred, the strange cat roused itself. It trotted after her into the kitchen and sniffed enquiringly at Lucy's saucer.

Mary checked a silent cry of protest. Poor thing — it had a right to food and drink. And of course it couldn't help not being Lucy.

She opened the pantry door to take out some milk, then swung round, startled, as she heard the sound of footsteps outside the back door.

No doubt about it — she was a bit jumpy on her own at nights . . .

Who could it be, she wondered. It couldn't be Flo — so early . . .

But it was.

Next moment, Flo was standing in the doorway, clutching her handbag which, if she'd been lucky, contained her bingo winnings, and the big shopping-bag which went with her everywhere.

Flo glanced at the cat which sat by Lucy's saucer, and for once in her life she seemed speechless.

"I found that address," Mary faltered half-guiltily. "Only the cat . . . the cat wasn't Lucy. But I thought . . ."

She broke off quickly. Something was moving in that huge, old shopping-bag of Flo's. Mary watched the bag like someone in a dream as out of it peeped the small clown-face of Lucy.

Half laughing, half crying, Mary pounced on the bag and lifted Lucy out, cradling the soft, warm, familiar body in her arms. Dimly, she heard Flo's voice: "When will you ever learn to use your eyes, Mary?"

Flo picked up the evening paper and with a flourish, thrust it triumphantly under her sister's nose.

"See what it says at the end of the Lost and Found column? You were in such a tizzy that you never even noticed."

Trembling, Mary looked at the paper. Found — small black female cat — smudges of white on nose and tummy, she read.

"I spotted it as soon as you'd left the house," Flo told her. "And it was obvious that it was Lucy."

"And — you fetched her . . . Oh, Flo — I don't know how to thank you . . ."

Brushing her sister's grateful thanks aside, Flo turned away abruptly. She seemed, Mary thought, a little embarrassed.

"Well, for one thing you can put the kettle on," Flo said, with a return to her customary brusqueness.

Lucy was purring now, her chin on Mary's shoulder. Mary fondled her, crooning words of love and welcome. Then she remembered the tea and, reluctantly, she put her down at last.

Next moment Lucy and the other cat confronted one another over the saucer, with looks of unmistakable suspicion.

Mary glanced at Flo and Flo glanced back at Mary. Then suddenly their lips began to twitch and soon the two sisters both began to shake with laughter.

Flo paused and wiped her eyes. "Looks like we're landed with the pair of them . . . oh dear, you'll be the death of me, our Mary . . ."

She began to fill the teapot. "Ah, well — just give them time and they'll settle down . . ."

Mary nodded in a glow of sheer contentment. Her kitchen, which only an hour ago had seemed so bleak, so empty, now seemed as cosy a place as she could wish for. And the tea was hot and strong and comforting.

As for the cats . . .

She smiled to herself, remembering her husband's words about two females in one kitchen . . .

But strangely enough, she wasn't really worried. Somehow she knew the cats would settle down together. Exactly as she and Flo would.

Given time. ■

Make Do And Mend

by Marion Naylor

Her mother's generation had been brought up to do
that. But these days, did her circumstances reflect
past training — or present necessity?

W HAT do you do at your meetings, Mum?" nine-year-old Emma enquired, sipping her cocoa slowly. "Talk mainly, darling," Isobel said briefly. "We try to think of ways of raising money to make life easier for old people — especially the ones who live on their own, and are poor."

Emma nodded knowingly. "Like Gran. She's old, and she lives on her own. Is she poor, as well?"

Tom rustled his paper. "Not judging by the presents she's forever spoiling you with!"

Isobel laughed. "Bedtime. Drink up."

A busy few days followed. There was the bring-and-buy to organise and the next concert — and so Isobel didn't give another thought to what Emma had said until a week later.

As her mother lived forty miles away, Isobel usually drove over to see her every Wednesday. They had a bit of lunch together and a gossip and Isobel found it relaxing to slip back into being a daughter again, cosseted and pampered.

Today, they sat on companionably over the empty plates with their elbows on the table and their hands cradling second cups of tea. Isobel's arm slipped, and some tea sloshed on to the tablecloth. "Sorry," she said, dabbing at it with her hankie.

Her mother laughed. "A drop of tea won't hurt that old cloth — it's seen far worse than that in its time."

For the first time Isobel looked objectively at the familiar seersucker cloth with its faded red and yellow squares. How long had it been on the go? It was so thin now and a couple of inches from her elbow she noticed a neat square patch had been carefully grafted into the pattern.

"Didn't it used to be bigger?" she asked, idly.

Her mother nodded. Her eyes looked back into the past. "When you were all at home we needed the leaf out in the table, and this cloth covered the whole thing. I always used to think it looked so cheerful . . ."

It didn't look cheerful now. It looked dingy. "I knew it would still do a turn so I cut off the end pieces where it had frayed and used the good bit of patching, but you can still see a faint purply stain, can't you? One of you spilled some blackcurrant juice and it never really came out.

"But it'll last a while yet, and when it's done it'll make some grand dusters. You know — make do and mend, love."

Make do and mend. It was just the way her mother's generation were brought up. It was then that she remembered Emma's words: "Is Gran poor?" She felt a sudden jolt.

Did her mother's circumstances reflect past training, or present necessity?

It was extraordinary difficult to stand apart and see your own mother as others might see her. Isobel looked across the table now and tried.

There was the familiar wise face and the gentle, kind eyes with laughter wrinkles at the corners.

Looking closely there were far more lines than she'd realised. Old, then, yes. Living alone, now, certainly. But poor?

Today her mother was wearing a comfortable weekday blouse and skirt. Her jumper wasn't the most flattering to her mother's colouring — a sort of dismal moss green. With a shock of new understanding, Isobel realised it had once been her father's.

"PENNY for them?" Isobel blinked. "I was just thinking," she said, truthfully, "what a clever make-do-and-mender you are."

They both gazed round the room, her mother with a contented smile on her face and Isobel with a growing realisation of what lay behind the shabby, comfortable room she'd taken so much for granted.

The threadbare carpet that had been down for ages somehow retaining its pattern even though its original colours had faded. The misshapen bit of pottery — intended for a vase — that Isobel had once made at school still leaned at a precarious angle on the sideboard. And the cushion covers, washed and put back on again straight away were fraying badly at the edges. Her mother had crocheted them from odd bits of leftover wool in uneven and discordant colours.

A fine daughter she was, Isobel thought self-critically; sitting on committees to make life more comfortable for the elderly, not even noticing that her own mother was struggling to keep her head above water.

"Mum," she said, hesitantly, as they settled down with another cup of tea, "How are you — for money, I mean? Are you managing all right?"

"Me? Gracious, yes." The kind, faded eyes widened expressively. "I'm managing fine. I've more than enough dear — there's no need to worry about me." Looking around at her shabby surroundings, it occurred to Isobel that her mother afforded the frequent generous presents to her family by denying herself. She sacrificed her own needs in order to give so selflessly to them . . . things would have to change . . .

"Goodness, look at the time . . ." Isobel said suddenly, glancing at her watch. She got to her feet. "I must get back for Emma coming home."

Her mother put her head on one side to see the time. It was such an automatic movement that up until now, it had gone unnoticed. But now, Isobel was seeing everything with fresh eyes.

"I suppose you must." Her mother straightened her head again. The clock stood in the centre of the mantelpiece, but it lay keeled over on its side.

Her father had tried to mend it once when it had stopped but, not being mechanically-minded, he'd had only partial success. It went, afterwards, but only in that one position. And today, spurred into action by her daughter's chance remark about her gran being poor, Isobel realised now why her mother went on cocking her head to consult a horizontal clock. A pension and her modest savings didn't run to new clocks as well as presents for her family. Or even to new cushion covers and tablecloths . . .

THOUGHTFULLY she drove home. At least the problem had been identified, but the solution was slightly more difficult. It was a matter of tactfully helping to replace worn-out furnishings without making her mother feel she was suddenly an object of charity.

That was why Isobel started in a small way.

"Isn't that lovely!" Her mother's pleasure was obvious the following week when Isobel casually handed her a new but roughly folded green and white tablecloth. "Just picked it up in a sale," she said, gratified at her success.

The following Sunday, when they were all over for tea, the new cloth was on the table. It went beautifully with Gran's best china, and Isobel was emboldened to hand over the other blue and white tablecloth she'd bought the day before.

"I managed to pick up another one — ridiculously low prices! You needn't go on patching up the old one now you've got two, Mother."

The replacement clock was a bit different, however. Luckily it was her mother's birthday a week or so later. She positively beamed with delight when she ripped off the wrapping to expose the delicate gilt clock.

GRADUALLY, over the next few months, the living-room was slowly transformed — in little ways, anyway.

Most Wednesdays Isobel contrived to bring some contribution, however small, like the sculptured onyx "organiser" for bits and pieces instead of the lurching pot.

And the set of toning cushion covers. "From the market," she explained. "Practically giving them away, they were!"

Her ingenuity was strained to the limit. But the only time she actually told lies, as opposed to merely exaggerating, was when she handed over a couple of smart, cotton sweaters in soft, glowing colours.

"I bought them for myself," she explained, feeling her face flush slightly, "but they're too small and I can't take them back as I've lost the receipt. You have them, Mum," she said.

Isobel thought it well worth the white lies for, next Wednesday, her mother greeted her wearing the rose-coloured one. It made her look years younger.

So far, so good. The larger items, though, were going to be a problem, but Isobel was already working on them. Take the worn carpet, for example.

Perhaps the best idea would be for her and Tom to buy a new carpet square, then after it had been down a week or two they could make out that the colour just didn't look right with the rest of the room, and persuade her mother she'd be doing them a favour if she took it off their hands . . .

Isobel smiled. There were all sorts of possibilities and ways round things to make her mother's house less dingy and shabby . . .

One Monday night the secretary of the old people's welfare committee rang up. "I'm awfully sorry, but something's come up and we've decided to move the meeting forward — Wednesday — one-thirty. Will that suit you? I know it's short notice, but I hope you'll —"

Isobel considered. "That's all right. Yes, I'll be there." I'll slip up to Mother's tomorrow instead, she decided.

Well, her arrival would be nice surprise, like the china teapot Isobel had bought recently and was bringing with her to replace the chipped and dribbling one her mother had put up with for years.

"It's only me, Mum!" she called as she let herself in with her key and hurried up the narrow hall and into the kitchen. "I'm a day early this week, hope you don't mind —"

At the sound of her voice her mother turned round, duster in hand. Instantly, her face broke into a smile of pleasure, then she flushed and looked guilty. Isobel was puzzled.

It didn't take Isobel long to realise why. For a start, Mum was her old familiar self, in her old familiar moss green jumper. The patched seersucker cloth was back on the table, the ancient crocheted cushion covers were back on. Even the drunken pot was on display again.

The gilt clock was still sparkling, but on the bookcase. In the middle of the mantelpiece, in the place of honour, the old wooden one was stretched out full length as if it hadn't ever got up.

There was an embarrassed pause. "You took me by surprise," the older woman said at last.

And then suddenly she started to laugh. "Oh, dear, I'm so sorry. Don't be upset — it's ever so kind of you, to bring me all these lovely new things. I know I'm lucky, really I do.

"It's just that —" She waved a hand around the room. "— the old things are — well, dear friends. Living memories . . .

"The cushion covers, for instance. See that bright red? That was a bit of your pram blanket — and the pink it clashes with was part of a skirt your granny knitted for me!

"As for that bright green, it makes me laugh to look at it.

"It was the wool from a bathing costume I knitted that practically fell off the first time it got wet . . ." She patted her dowdy jumper affectionately. "And your dad lived in this green jumper —"

When Isobel reached home, she was still chuckling to herself.

"Where've you been today, Mum?" Emma asked tucking into her tea.

"I've been to Gran's. And I've learned a lot."

Emma looked up and said gravely, "About Gran? Is she really poor?"

"Poor?" Isobel echoed her daughter's words. "You know something, Emma — Gran's richer than anybody would ever guess." ■

Meet My Mum...

by Sheila Ireland

Julie and his mother were getting on famously — so why was Edward still so anxious . . . ?

A S he drove, Edward Hammond was thinking how good it would be if his mother took an instant liking to his girlfriend, Julie Wells. Of course, he didn't have to worry. Foolish even to think about it, really.

He had always taken his girlfriends home to meet his mother and she always welcomed them with open arms and a warm smile.

He just hoped she wouldn't bring out his baby pictures. Or say he was losing weight and was he eating properly? Or fuss over him like he was six years old. Or call him Teddy, which he knew she would.

"And your mother never thought about getting married again?" Julie asked, picking up the conversation of a minute ago.

She was sitting alongside him in the red MG and they were whizzing along the country road on their way to his mother's cottage in Cornwall.

The sun was shining and Julie was wearing a smart, yet feminine dress in lilac. Her dark hair looked glossy and soft.

Edward thought she looked gorgeous — but there was nothing unusual in that — she always looked gorgeous. Even so, he knew she'd taken especial care with her appearance today — for his mum's sake.

That only made him love her more.

"No. I don't think so," he said. "There were other blokes, dates and things, you know, but nothing serious. She seems happy enough, though."

"Such a long time, to be alone."

"Hey, I was there, remember." Edward acted peeved, then grinned.

Julie punched him playfully on the arm. "No, Ed, you know what I mean. It must have been hard for her, losing your father so young." Her blue eyes were serious.

"I don't know, Julie," he said honestly. "I was only three, remember, when he died."

"She must have loved him very much."

"She did," he replied quietly. "You only have to hear her talk."

"And he must have loved her, Ed."

Edward steered the car carefully around a bend in the road. "I hardly remember my dad," he said. "But Mum says I only have to look in the mirror to know what he looked like.

"You'll see when we get home. Mum's wedding picture's got pride of place in the lounge."

THEY drove on down the road, and they talked almost non-stop, as if they were nervous or something.

Edward laughed. "This is crazy," he told her. "Mum really is nice — she'll fall over herself to make you welcome. There's nothing to worry about . . ."

And it was true. His mother had always gone out of her way to be friendly, generous and kind to his girlfriends. He smiled at the memories.

She had also been patient, for there had been lots of girlfriends, stretching back to his days at university.

Blondes and brunettes and redheads. Quiet girls and garrulous girls, tall girls and short girls, good-looking girls and plain girls, and bright and ambitious girls who would go places and did.

Somehow he'd never got around to marrying any of them.

Julie started to talk about her own family.

Edward got on well with her parents and last time he'd been there, her younger sister, Pam, had persuaded him to play Scrabble. They'd all joined in and it had been great fun.

"I think she has a crush on you," Julie teased him, remembering.

Edward grinned, unabashed. In fact, he felt quite flattered by the thought. "The feeling's mutual . . . I think I'm going to like having a sister . . ."

"Weren't you lonely being an only child?" Julie asked suddenly.

He laughed and shook his head. "No. Mum made sure of that. She even used to play football with me! Besides, I had lots of school-friends.

"Mum used to bake cakes and biscuits and all sorts." He laughed again. "Everybody always ended up at our house."

"She sounds lovely," Julie sighed. "You're very close, aren't you?"

Edward nodded. "Best mum in the world! Mum and Dad, when you think about it. She's great."

They were at the top of a hill overlooking the sea. They heard the waves crashing and the shrieking of seagulls.

"We'll be there in about half an hour," Edward said and smiled.

"Happy?" Julie said.

"Couldn't be happier," he said truthfully, and drove on.

HE was thinking about the last thing his mother always said after a week end visit when he had to return to his job and his flat in London.

She would say, "Be happy, son," and hug him, and he would say, "What else?" and laugh.

He never told her that it was sometimes very hard to be happy or that he often failed and the feelings of failure could last for weeks.

There was no rhyme or reason for it, either. It was too vague and whimsical. Quite silly, really, that a man of 29 should actually begin to wonder if he was never meant to marry.

It just seemed odd to him that all of his friends had wives and families of their own and he had none — just girlfriends. He wondered what his father would have said.

"Look, Ed!" Julie turned to him, excited. "The signpost. Three miles to Edgemarton!" Her face was flushed and her eyes shone as she smiled at him and put her hand on his shoulder.

He was glad she was there, beside him, and he told himself he was sure his mother would like her.

In any case, he hoped everything would go well because it was Julie's idea to come for the weekend. She said she had heard so much about his mother that she jolly well wanted to meet her. What was wrong with that?

Nothing, of course. It was just him. Him and a vague feeling that he couldn't put into words and which was probably foolish.

Yet he had wondered if he had done the right thing, over the years, in bringing his girlfriends home to meet his mother.

He'd wondered if it were possible that a boy who had grown up without a father and whose mother was generous and kind and loving, might in some way be different from others.

Maybe such a lad could become more attached to his mother, and she to him?

Nonsense, of course. Psychological twaddle, not worth thinking about. Yet he had missed never having a father to sit down and talk to man-to-man about the world . . . life.

He had never witnessed everyday affection shown by a man towards the woman he loved — never known how much his father loved his mother.

So much wondering, and then Julie had come along and all of those thoughts had faded and disappeared like smoke in the wind . . .

It was only today, now, that the wondering began again. He looked across at Julie and she smiled, her eyes full of love and he felt warm and good.

But he couldn't deny his feeling of nervousness or the tension in his hands on the wheel, or the thought that if he had never known love, how could he be certain he had found it at last with Julie?

It worried him, but there was nothing at all he could do — just wait . . .

"Now sit yourselves down, Julie, Teddy." Catherine Hammond beamed and ushered them to the two big green comfy seats by the fireplace.

"Isn't it lovely down here when the sun's out?" she said to Julie. "Excuse me a minute. I'll just fetch the tea." She hurried out of the room to the kitchen.

Julie raised and lowered her eyebrows and smiled. "She's nice," she whispered.

Edward had noticed that his mother had been to the hairdresser's for the occasion, as she always did when he brought his girlfriends down for the weekend.

"Can't have them thinking your mum's scruffy, can we?" she always said, but Edward had a notion that it was because she didn't quite know what to expect and it helped fortify her, no matter what.

She was slim, with elegant grey streaks in her fine dark hair and her surprisingly youthful face was both lively and gentle. She wore her best dress and the pearls his father had given her on their wedding day.

That confirmed she was definitely determined to make a good impression.

LATER Edward told himself to try to relax and just to let the day run its course. There was nothing to be gained in paying so much attention to what his mother might say or do.

Yet he couldn't help himself. There was a bond between himself and his mother which he could not easily shrug off or ignore.

She had, after all, helped and advised and guided him through his childhood and his life and he had never doubted her. His happiness had always come first, as had hers with him.

It was a natural loyalty, but today it worried and confused him.

He felt curiously tense as he watched his mother talk to Julie and smile the same welcoming smile and ask the same friendly questions she had asked all the other girls in the past.

Finally, he stood up and excused himself and went out into the garden.

The air was fresh and he was glad to stand there and look out at the green, faraway hills for a long moment.

He was remembering all the other girls, and how he'd thought he loved each and every one of them, and nothing had come of it.

He recalled how, after each of them had left and gone out of his life and he stood silently at home wondering, his mother would come up to him and say comfortingly, "She wasn't right for you, Teddy. She wasn't the one . . ."

He never doubted it. He believed her, and because it was true he was able to get over it and get on with his life.

Only today, it was Julie.

Edward stared at the faraway hills and he knew this time it was right. He had never been more sure.

Yet he couldn't dismiss his mother's face from his mind or her voice saying, "Teddy, she isn't right. Julie isn't the one for you . . ."

And he wondered what he would do, if she did.

"Teddy." His mother called to him from the house. "There's another cup of tea, fresh, if you like."

"Coming, Mum," he said and walked slowly back.

THIS time he watched and listened more closely, as he sat in the big comfortable chair in the small house.

He could feel the closeness and cosiness of the place and the tension began to leave him. It had been right to come home, to bring Julie with him, no matter what.

Julie liked his mother, he was sure of that. And his mother seemed to like Julie.

He thought he could see it in the way she spoke and smiled and touched Julie's hand, and even in the way the tears came to her eyes when they looked at her wedding photograph and Julie said, "Ed, it's amazing, your father looks just like you!"

He was aware of his mother's affection for Julie later, as well, and he even noticed a difference in himself, when his mother inevitably brought out the family album and began showing Julie his baby pictures.

This time there was no sense of embarrassment. He even managed to join in the laughter and talk about the scrapes he had got into and the things his mother had had to put up with.

There were pictures of his mum playing football and he heard Julie and his mother giggling together as he went out to the kitchen to fetch the bottle of sherry and the glasses.

Everything's all right, he told himself. It's OK.

Even so, he could still feel the tension in his shoulders and he rubbed the back of his neck with his hand.

It would be so good if it was different this time. If his mother was being more than just kind and polite and generous. But he was just too anxious to know one way or another.

When his mother came into the kitchen behind him, he was pouring the drinks and didn't turn round.

Instead, he simply stared down at the glasses, holding his breath.

His mother walked to his side and frowned a little as she looked at him before she said softly, so that Julie couldn't hear, "Teddy, if you were smart you'd ask that girl to marry you."

He smiled then and said quietly, "I did, Mum. Yesterday."

His mother's face stilled and the seriousness in her eyes faded to softness. She put her hand on his.

"Teddy, I'm so happy for you," she said, and there was a huskiness in her voice.

"I just knew it was different with Julie. The minute you walked through the door, I knew."

"Oh?" Edward was puzzled.

His mother's eyes were misty. "You see, son, you were looking at Julie just the way your father used to look at me, all those years ago. I'll never forget . . ."

It was almost midnight and none of them felt in the least bit tired, not Julie nor his mum nor himself.

Edward sighed softly. He knew there would be other special moments in his life, but he would always remember this one.

Julie was sitting on the couch with his mother, chatting and smiling and it was as if they had known each other all their lives. And as he looked at her, he became aware of a feeling of joy that was almost overwhelming.

He let his eyes drift upwards, to his mother's wedding picture on the wall above them.

And the realisation came then — like a whisper — and suddenly he knew exactly how much his father had loved his mother. ∎

FRIENDS & NEIGHBOURS

by Shirley Worrell

That's all they were to each other. But if he
could earn her trust, perhaps, in time,
he might win her heart, too . . .

AS soon as Richard saw his new neighbour, he thought all his dreams had come true. The house next-door to his had been empty for twelve months and Richard had watched the grass grow taller and the weeds grow stronger as the weeks went by.

As soon as he'd seen the estate agent triumphantly hammer a Sold sign into the ground. Richard had started to wonder about his new neighbours.

He'd hoped they'd at least be friendly, but he hadn't dared to hope for a neighbour like the girl who climbed out of her car the next day and let herself into the empty house.

Tall and slim, with bouncing fair hair and a skip in her step, he knew immediately that she was the girl of his dreams.

Richard was standing at the kitchen window when he saw her arrive. After changing into a clean shirt, he went outside to loiter in his front garden, hoping for another glimpse.

While he pretended to inspect the rose bushes, his mind was busy with plans for getting to know his new neighbour.

Maybe he could invite her to have lunch at his place . . . or ask her if she'd like to try the new restaurant in town.

He could offer to check the electrics in her new home . . . or help to move furniture . . .

Hearing her front door close, Richard turned around so as to be ready to introduce himself. She was striding down the path, seemingly unaware that he was there, so he called out, "Hello!"

She stopped and looked straight at him. "Hello," she replied.

Richard walked across to the fence. "I'm Richard Knight, your neighbour."

She seemed to force a smile to her lips. "Mrs Carpenter."

The emphasis on the "Mrs" was so heavy that Richard's dreams suddenly sank to his toes. For confirmation, he looked at her left hand and saw a narrow circle of gold shining in the morning sun.

"Nice to have met you, Mr Knight," she called out, already walking towards her car.

Richard watched her drive away, taking his dreams with her. He should have known she was married. It had all seemed too good to be true.

He consoled himself with the knowledge that she wasn't as friendly as she looked. In fact, that brief meeting had been distinctly chilly.

For the next few days, Richard tried to forget about the cool Mrs Carpenter, but when he returned from work on Friday evening, he saw that her car was parked outside the house.

A quick glance told him that her furniture was installed, and he wondered if Mr Carpenter had taken up residence, too.

THE next morning, Richard awoke to the sound of a lawn mower. He wandered over to the window, expecting to see his first glimpse of Mr Carpenter.

But it wasn't Mr Carpenter who was struggling with the small electric mower — it was Mrs Carpenter. And she looked more lovely than ever, Richard thought wistfully.

He skipped breakfast and went out to his back garden where, on the other side of the fence, Mrs Carpenter was persevering with a mower that just wasn't powerful enough to cut through the long grass.

"Need any help?" Richard shouted over the fence.

She switched off the mower and treated Richard to her cool smile.

"Good morning, Mr Knight."

"Please, call me Richard," he insisted.

"Richard," she repeated.

He waited, but it seemed he was still to call her Mrs Carpenter.

"Would you like me to run my mower over it?" Richard asked. "It has more power than that one."

"No. No, really. Thanks, but I can manage."

Richard couldn't see how. "It's no trouble," he assured her. "I was going to do mine anyway."

She hesitated, clearly not wanting to accept his offer but knowing she was fighting a losing battle with the grass.

"I'll bring it round," Richard said, before she could argue any more.

"I'll have to get a new mower," she said when he came back. "Would you recommend this make?"

"It's ideal," Richard assured her, adding, "If Mr Carpenter wants to try it out before deciding to buy one, he's very welcome."

Richard was surprised to see two bright spots of colour fly to her face. "He works abroad," she explained quickly, "so I'll be doing the garden."

Richard acknowledged a glow of pleasure at the thought of Mr Carpenter being abroad, but he quickly dismissed it. Having a husband in some foreign country made her no less married.

"The mower's always in the shed," Richard told her. "Feel free to use it any time."

She was about to speak when two young boys wandered into the garden. They eyed Richard curiously.

"Hello." Richard smiled. "My name's Richard. I live next door." He gestured to his house.

Mrs Carpenter then introduced her two sons.

Matthew was eight and Andrew six, and Richard couldn't remember ever meeting such well-mannered children. Almost too well-mannered, he thought, if that were possible. There didn't seem to be any sense of mischief about them at all.

A S the weeks passed, Richard thought the elusive Mr Carpenter might pay his family a visit, but there was no sign of the man.

Richard didn't see much of Mrs Carpenter either, but he did learn that her name was Joanna. She didn't volunteer the information but Richard overheard Tom, their postman, call out, "Morning, Joanna. Lovely day."

She was all smiles for Tom, Richard noticed. Occasionally, if Richard were lucky, he'd get a reluctant smile from her but, more often than not, she was polite but distant.

Sometimes Richard watched her playing with the children in the garden. With them, she was carefree and full of fun.

He began to think he must have done something to offend her — after all, she was friendly towards other people.

Richard couldn't fault her behaviour, for she was always polite, but the warmth she showed others evaporated when she saw him.

Thankfully her children were far more approachable. They always made a beeline for Richard, and he enjoyed chatting to them.

The three of them often spent half an hour kicking a football over the low fence that divided their two gardens, and it was during one of these sessions that Richard mentioned the football season was starting again and that he was going to watch the local team that afternoon.

"Do you go to every game?" Matthew wanted to know.

"I never miss one if I can help it," Richard replied.

The two faces that stared at him across the fence were clearly filled with envy.

Now Richard didn't know what to do. He was unsure if he should offer to take them to the game, but he could see how desperately they wanted to go.

Hang it all, he thought suddenly. If their own father isn't around to take them out, then why shouldn't someone else?

With his conscience only vaguely troubled at the thought of how Joanna would react, Richard said, "Tell you what, if your mum says it's OK, you can come with me. Would you like that?"

As for liking it, they could hardly believe it! "Can we?" they asked together.

"As long as your mum agrees," Richard replied, knowing that she could do little but agree now.

Before he could say anything else, the two boys were shouting at the tops of their voices, "Mum! Mum! Quick!"

Seconds later, Joanna flew out of the house.

"I mentioned to Matthew and Andrew that I was going to a football match this afternoon," Richard explained carefully. "They're more than welcome to come along if it's OK with you."

"Please, Mum," Andrew begged. "Please say we can."

"We've never been to a real game," Matthew put in. "We can go, can't we? Please, Mum!"

Joanna looked from the boys to Richard and then back to the boys. Richard could see that she wanted to say no and so avoid any involvement with him, but she also knew it would break the boys' hearts.

"They'll be quite safe," Richard assured her. "It's a far cry from the

Premier League, but it's good football. And there's never any crowd trouble."

"But are you sure you don't mind?" she asked, frowning.

"I'll enjoy the company."

"It's very kind of you, Mr — Richard — and I know they'll love every minute of it." She hesitated then smiled. "OK, boys, but you must behave. Do exactly as Richard tells you . . ."

THEY arrived at the ground early and Richard bought them each a programme.

"Why don't mothers take you to football games?" Matthew asked. "They only ever take you to shops or parks."

"Most women aren't really interested in football!" Richard smiled.

"Then it's not fair," Andrew decided. "Just because we haven't got a proper dad, we don't get to go anywhere good!"

Andrew had echoed Richard's mental picture of the absent Mr Carpenter. He was far from being a "proper dad".

"I'm sure your father's very busy," he told the boys, not sure of any such thing. "Maybe he'll take you to all the best places when he comes home."

Matthew shook his head. "We don't see him," he said with a shrug. "We've only seen him once since him and Mum got divorced."

Divorced? The word flashed back and forth in Richard's mind.

"I see," Richard said, not seeing at all. "I didn't realise your parents were divorced."

"Dad wanted to marry someone else," Andrew explained, as if it were the most natural thing in the world.

Richard was surprised into admiration for the boys who had dismissed their father in a couple of sentences and who now had their minds on the crowd gathering to watch the game.

Richard's feelings for Mr Carpenter hit an all-time high. He could feel himself shaking with anger. He wished the man had never been born!

"Right," he announced briskly, "if you're going to support this team properly, you need a team scarf — and as big a rosette as possible."

He took them to the small souvenir shop and when the game started, they were both waving their scarves excitedly.

Richard was aware of their "oohs" and "aahs" throughout the match but if questioned, he wouldn't have known what the score was. All he could think of was Joanna.

Suddenly he had dozens of reasons for her cool attitude towards him.

Perhaps being married to a man like her ex-husband had put her off men for life — and who could blame her?

Perhaps she still loved her ex-husband and didn't even notice other men. But she couldn't love a man like that — could she?

He hated to think of her and the boys being abandoned but gradually his anger faded. Joanna wasn't married at all. She was free!

B ACK home, the boys rushed inside, leaving Richard to bring up the rear. "It was great, Mum!" Matthew cried. "Really great. And look, we've got proper scarves and rosettes!"

"We could see everything," Andrew joined in.

"And did you behave yourselves?" Joanna asked, smiling at their excitement.

"Yes," Richard answered for them. "We've enjoyed ourselves."

"Thank you, Richard," Joanna said quietly. "I really appreciate it."

"I enjoyed their company, Mrs Carpenter."

"My name's Joanna."

Richard was momentarily taken aback, but then he smiled. "I know."

She blushed but returned the smile, convincing Richard that Mr Carpenter was either blind or stupid, and quite probably both.

"I've got a casserole in the oven," Joanna went on, regaining a little of her composure. "There's more than enough for four and you're very welcome to share it with us if you'd like to."

Richard quickly accepted before she changed her mind.

Joanna chatted a lot during the meal, telling Richard about her work as a freelance translator.

She spoke fluent German, French and Spanish and had a smattering of Russian. Richard was impressed.

"I was always interested in languages — even at school," Joanna replied with a self-effacing smile.

She smiled frequently, Richard noticed, and if the reserve was still there, it was receding.

He knew she'd been hurt in the past, and that she'd be wary of starting a relationship with any man, but he felt sure that they were slowly becoming friends.

When it was time for him to leave, Joanna thanked him once again on behalf of the boys.

"They seem to miss out on things like that," she added. "When I told you that my husband worked abroad — well, he does work abroad, but he's not my husband any more. We're divorced."

"I know," Richard admitted. "The boys told me." He wasn't sure what else to say and his quiet, "I'm sorry," sounded very inadequate.

"Don't be," Joanna replied. "I was young and made a mistake.

"But I don't regret my marriage, because I have Matthew and Andrew. And we're happy."

A hint of reserve was creeping into her voice so Richard quickly thanked her for the meal and returned to his house.

It would take time for Joanna to feel at ease with any man, he thought, but he had all the time in the world. And all the patience she needed . . .

★ ★ ★ ★

Things went better than he'd dared to hope, and they soon fell into a routine. Richard took Matthew and Andrew to the football each Saturday and always stayed for a meal afterwards. Then he and Joanna would sit and talk for hours.

Gradually, they became a foursome, often going on outings together at the weekends.

They were a foursome, Richard often thought, but they weren't a family . . .

He knew that one day Joanna might tell him that she was moving away, or that she'd met someone she wanted to marry.

He knew that one day, Joanna and the boys could drift out of his life leaving him with nothing but memories.

And if he lost them now, Richard didn't know what he'd do.

He and Joanna were friends, good friends, but did she want anything more than friendship? At times Richard thought she might but until he was sure, he didn't want to push the issue and frighten her off.

THEN, one Saturday, he and the boys returned from a football match to find Joanna in the kitchen.

"Did you win?" she asked with a smile.

"We deserved to." Richard grinned. "But the ref badly needed an appointment with the optician."

Matthew and Andrew shrieked with laughter and Matthew piped up, "And the man behind us called him a —"

Richard clamped his hand over Matthew's mouth just in time. "I don't think your mother wants to hear what he called him. It wasn't very polite, was it?"

Looking at Joanna he explained sheepishly, "It was said in the heat of the moment."

The boys were heading for their bedrooms when Matthew called out with a cheeky laugh, "It was true, though."

Before Richard could say anything, Joanna reached up and kissed him on the cheek. "Thanks, Richard."

Without conscious thought, Richard's hands went to her waist, halting her escape. He felt her stiffen and immediately thought he'd made a big mistake. He'd turned one brief, meaningless kiss into a very difficult moment.

He didn't want to let her go and have the awkwardness remain between them so he tried to make light of it.

"Thanks for what? For introducing your sons to the finer points of the English language?"

She laughed and made no attempt to escape him. "Thanks for being so good with them." She looked straight at him and added quietly, "I hope they don't make a nuisance of themselves. You do realise that they've selected you for their new father?"

"I have noticed the odd hint being dropped," Richard admitted with a smile.

Joanna laughed softly. "Odd hint? All I hear about is how brilliant you are at everything. And you work in a very smart office so you must have lots of money. And your car's better than ours."

"What more could a girl want?" Richard joked. "They constantly remind me of how pretty you are and what a good cook you are."

"And that's the sum total of my talents?" Joanna groaned.

Richard still had his hands on her waist, and he didn't want to let her go. Ever.

"I don't have the heart to tell them they're wasting their time," he murmured. "You see, I've been sold on you from the very first moment I saw you."

Feeling he was treading on dangerous ground, he forced a teasing note into his voice. "Even if you were the most unfriendly neighbour I've ever known."

"I was, wasn't I?" Joanna sighed. "It's just that if you're divorced, men think you're so lonely that you'll consider it a favour if they so much as smile in your direction.

"And then there are the men who immediately think you're looking for husband number two and run a mile. Either way, it causes a lot of unpleasantness."

"And which category was I put in?" Richard teased.

"I decided that you were just a good neighbour." She smiled. "Although I sometimes wonder if you got more than you bargained for," she added.

"We've started to treat you like a permanent feature, haven't we? Is that what you want, Richard?"

Richard gazed at her for long moments as he thought out an answer. He could see now that she wasn't about to run away. What they were feeling had grown from trust and they could be completely honest with each other.

"I want everything," he said simply. "I want you to be my wife. I want your sons to be our sons. I want us to be a real family. But," he added, "I'll take whatever you're prepared to give."

Joanna moved closer and slipped her arms around his neck. "I want everything, too," she whispered.

And when Richard kissed her, he knew that his dreams really had come true. ■

Mark's picture of the forge brought back long forgotten
memories. When I was between the ages of seven and
fourteen we lived in a house ten doors away from a forge.
I had to pass it to and from school. I knew better than to linger
and adore the horses in the morning but on the way home
I always stopped and was often chivvied away . . . I adored
those wonderful horses, especially the huge brewery horses
which inspired me many years later to
write Breed of Giants.

DALLYING

Hurry home from school, they said.
We worry when you're late.
But I could never pass the forge
Just ten doors from our gate.
The fire blazed fierce,
The iron shoes glowed.
There was the lovely pony some children rode.
And there the glorious coal black horses
That pranced in front of the funeral hearses.
The milkman's Prince, the grocer's George,
All of them came to be shod at the forge.
Most of all I loved the giant grey,
One of four that pulled the brewery dray.
Her brown eyes shone, her mane was silk,
Her gleaming coat the colour of milk.
Into the water the glowing shoes hiss . . .

The spell is broken. The Smith says, "Miss,
It's time to go and you'd better hurry.
It's getting late and your folks will worry."
No more Smith and his burning coals.
No more horses and skittish foals.
Yet now in memory I'm back in that lane
And the Smith is forging his shoes again.
And the bright eyes glow and the tails swish fast
And horse after horse goes galloping past.
I sit and dream of those days without care
And the petal soft coat of that lovely grey mare.

A poem by Joyce Stranger,
inspired by an illustration by Mark Viney.

Seeing Red

by
***Heather
Bennett***

*If my daughter wanted scarlet icing on her birthday
cake, scarlet it would be. But by the time I'd finished,
I was feeling decidedly blue. . .*

IT was all my sister-in-law, Nancy's fault. You know how some people
always say the wrong thing? Well, Nancy is just such a person. The
Cranby Clarion, my husband calls her, which is something of a slur on
that newspaper. The Clarion usually gets its facts right. Nancy never does.
Long-established friendships rock when she's around, happy marriages totter
— all because of information she has misheard, misunderstood
or misinterpreted.

Fortunately, when she left school, she chose to work in the local library,
where she could do little harm other than spoiling the readers' pleasure by
telling them exactly whodunit as she stamped their thrillers.

Had she decided on a career in international diplomacy, we'd probably be facing World War Twenty-three by now!

And questions! Nancy is the original question mark — and the more innocent the question, the more trouble it's likely to cause. That's the way it was with Rosie . . .

Rosie is my daughter, as dark, blue-eyed and beautiful as her aunt, but there the resemblance ends.

Rosie doesn't let her tongue run away with her. Her speech is terse and to the point — even monosyllabic at times.

Of course, this could have something to do with the fact that Rosie is not yet three years old, but I prefer to think it shows a natural restraint, learned in the cradle, from hearing the gaffes made by her Aunt Nancy.

The question Nancy asked seemed innocent enough. She called in for coffee yesterday, just three days before Rosie's third birthday. She asked Rosie about the planned party, then about the birthday cake.

Rosie gave her the look she saves for particularly stupid adults and told her it would have candles . . . three, of course.

"And what colour is it going to be?" Nancy asked.

"Red," Rosie said.

"Well, pink," I said quickly, thinking of the cake, already iced, waiting in the pantry. "That's pale red, I suppose."

"Red," Rosie repeated firmly, turning the withering look on me this time. "Not pink, red."

I gave Nancy a baleful look which she returned with a delicate shrug and the innocent smile that usually gets her out of trouble.

I don't know what you're annoyed about, that look said. It can't be anything I've said this time.

I ADDED a large bottle of cochineal to the shopping list, and as soon as Rosie was asleep that night I started work. "What are you doing?" my husband, Steve, asked incredulously as I carefully stripped the icing, pale as apple blossom, from the birthday cake.

Briefly, I told him. I can be terse, too. I managed to refer to my sister-in-law as "Nancy", avoiding — just — calling her "your sister."

He'd blushed for her too often to be a fair target.

"You're mad," he said. "Rosie'll have forgotten by morning."

Regretting my restraint, I gave him a look intended to be as withering as Rosie's. He got the message.

"Oh well," he muttered with a shrug, retreating behind the Clarion, "perhaps not."

I mixed creamy white icing in a bowl and reached for the bottle of cochineal. "Careful now," I told myself. "It's powerful stuff."

A few drops turned the mixture pale pink. A few more and it was the colour of candy-floss. Half a bottle and it was a deep, unappetising pink. Pink not red.

Shutting my mind to the thought of all those beetles whose lives had been cut prematurely short to grant my daughter's wish, I up-ended the bottle.

The colour deepened. The icing now looked totally inedible. But it still didn't look red.

Of course it's red, I told myself. You're getting paranoid. A second opinion will settle it.

"Carmine?" Steve hazarded. "Magenta? Fuchsia? Cyclamen?"

"What about red?" I stopped him before he could go through the whole rainbow.

He looked from the mess in the mixing bowl to me, torn between the truth and his desire to get off the hook.

"Well, sort of . . ." he said.

I thrust the bowl towards him and he flinched.

"Taste it," I said.

Reluctantly he did as I asked, transferring the smallest possible amount from bowl to finger to mouth.

"Well?"

"It's . . . there's a sort of bitterness . . . behind the sweetness," he said at last.

"Candy!" I called for the dog, whose name had been chosen because of her habit of begging for chocolate from the neighbourhood children and for her greed over anything sweet.

I dropped a generous dollop of the garish mixture into her bowl. She sniffed it suspiciously, eyed me reproachfully over her shoulder, and slunk out of the room.

My mouth set, I scooped the contents of the mixing-bowl into the sink and turned on the hot tap. Ironically, it did look red as it dissolved in bloody streams and ran down the wastepipe.

MY friend Jan next door came to the rescue with a glass of wine to calm my nerves, and a small bottle of red food colouring.

"This is what you need," she said knowledgeably, having been to a cake-icing demonstration last year. "This will turn anything scarlet. Just don't use too much, and don't spill it on anything, or you'll never get it out."

Suppressing the thought of what it was going to do to our insides, I thanked her profusely and hurried home, clutching the precious bottle and a borrowed packet of icing sugar, my own supplies having been exhausted.

Jane was right about its powerful nature. Within seconds I had a mixing bowl full of icing that was scarlet, brighter than poppies or pillarboxes or even Nancy's fingernails.

Triumphantly I slapped it on the denuded cake, smoothed it into place and replaced the candles and decorations on the top.

With the uncanny knack they both possess of knowing when it's safe to emerge, Steve and Candy came into the kitchen just as I finished.

"Do we have to eat it?" Steve asked, reeling at the sight of the cake, while Candy's tail stopped in mid wag.

"You don't," I said. "But I'll expect you to hold Nancy down while I force-feed her a very large slice!"

The next afternoon I took Rosie to visit Steve's parents. Although it was mid-September, the sun was warm and Mum and I sat outside drinking tea while Rosie and her grandfather went for a walk in the nearby woods.

We were still sitting there when they came back, Rosie's arms so full of flowers we could just see her blue eyes and a wisp of dark hair over the top.

"She gets more like our Nancy every day," Steve's mum said.

"Only in looks," I said firmly.

"Oh yes, it was in looks I meant," she agreed.

Rosie ran up to her gran and tipped the armful of wild bluebells into her lap, where they lay, like a pool of spilled sky.

"Lovely, aren't they, Rosie?" Gran said. "Do you know what colour they are?"

Rosie looked up at her, her dancing eyes, so like Nancy's, the exact colour of the flowers.

"Course I do," she said, in a tone that brooked no argument. "They're red, the same colour as my birthday cake is going to be." ■

The Problem With Parents

by Sheila Ireland

. . . is they always want to run your life — and occasionally end up making a better job of it!

MIKE JACKSON blinked at himself sleepily in the bathroom mirror. There are a lot of things you learn in the process of growing up. One is that you outgrow your parents . . .

Mike's mind was rambling, as it always did first thing in the morning.

Parents are like that. His mind went on rambling, as he recalled his mother's phone call, which had got him out of bed that morning. You get yourself safely through childhood and they still tell you what food to eat.

He added some toothpaste to his brush.

You become a senior at high school and they still want to help you with your homework, even when it's beyond them.

He plied the toothbrush with enthusiasm.

After you've taken your degree in Law and the Social Sciences and have become a partner in a nice, thriving practice, they still worry about the time you go to bed.

He sucked hard on his teeth and swallowed some of the pepperminty toothpaste.

When you're successful and have bought your own car and have your own home and a wife of your own, they still think they know what's best for you.

His lips and chin were covered in toothpaste froth and he pulled a face in the mirror..

Parents. They bring you up to be confident and able and self-reliant and when you do just that, they think you've double-crossed them.

That was all very well, he thought, as he took a last stab at his teeth, then sloshed his clean-shaven face with cold water, but they shouldn't interfere in his marriage. Or, to be more honest and precise, in the break-up of his marriage.

He splashed some aftershave on his face, draped a towel round his neck and walked back into the bedroom to begin getting dressed for the office.

Again it struck him, as it had every morning since Shelley had moved out, that the room didn't look right any more. It had an uncomfortable feel to it. Shelley's wardrobe and mirrored dressing table looked out of place, standing empty as they were.

He slipped on his shirt, took three deep breaths and felt better. He reminded himself to be zestful and switched-on and enthusiastic.

Today, he was 27 years old, so he had the right to be in a jolly, good and congratulatory mood.

It was a Red Letter Day for his parents, too, for it just happened to be their wedding anniversary — hence the phone call this morning to remind him not to forget their little dinner party this evening at eight.

If only they'd left it at that. But parents don't. No, with them there's always a proviso . . . they always have to go one better and spoil things.

"Yes, you can, if . . ." or, "All right, but . . ."

Or as his mother had said on the phone, "That's lovely, but don't you think it would be a good idea to stop all the nonsense and bring Shelley along?"

Nonsense indeed! Mike fixed his tie and pulled on his jacket with a shrug.

Of course, his parents were old-fashioned and he had to try to be patient and understanding. People of their generation couldn't be expected to know of the pressures that undermine a modern marriage.

He brushed and combed his hair, pursed his lips and tried to whistle, failed and left the house.

It was on his way to the office that he spotted Shelley. Confused, he looked abruptly away.

When he looked cautiously back, he realised he was mistaken. The girl didn't look at all like Shelley.

Anyway, what did he care, he asked himself, and walked on, not knowing why he had looked abruptly away.

What he did know and was thinking about was that Shelley hadn't sent him a birthday card.

THE office didn't know of his troubles with Shelley, though he had mentioned it to the senior partner, old Benjamin Daniels. Benjy, as everyone called him in private, had simply said, "Huummph, you young people, I don't know," and hadn't uttered a word on the subject since.

Mike was relieved. He didn't want gossipy Helen or amorous Delia to find out that Shelley had gone from his life.

He spent the morning on property-transference contracts and wondered about the wheelings and dealings of big business and how the small type in the contracts was so important.

It was this line of thinking that made him dial his mother's number, because had just remembered another thing that parents were, and that was cunning.

"Mother? Hi. About this evening . . . You haven't invited Shelley, have you? You wouldn't do that to me?

"No? Good. No, I don't think I'm being silly.

"Look, I just thought I'd better make sure. Goodbye, Mother. I'll see you tonight."

It was three days since Shelley had left him. He still couldn't understand it. Surely one full and blissful year of marriage could withstand a reasonable measure of argument . . . a touch of sarcasm, even a few sharp words and a bit of screaming and shouting?

So much for the argument that a good, loud, healthy row could do wonders for a marriage. The only effect it had had on Shelley was to make her pack her bags and walk out the door!

He had to admit he'd been a bit taken aback at the time. Shelley was intelligent: a sensible and undemonstrative person. The sight of her standing there, with two suitcases in her hands and tears misting her eyes that were still blazing mad at what she called his selfishness, had left him dumbstruck.

And all because he had said that it was better for them to splash out on a new car than to think about having a baby.

He had explained they were young and modern and if they were wise they would invest in a few luxuries now, when they could afford it.

"Is money all you think about?" Shelley had said grimly.

He had laughed at how tough she'd sounded, because she had always been lady-like and fair and even-tempered and more than willing to go along with anything he said.

Playfully, he'd pushed the argument back to her. He'd been affable, engagingly humorous, and thrown in a few jokes in an effort to make her smile.

It hadn't worked.

Shelley had burst into tears and called him selfish and uncaring. If he didn't want a family, well, that was all right, she'd said. Maybe they should never have got married in the first place!

One thing had led to another and before he knew it they were going at it hammer and tongs — having a rip-roaring slanging match, saying totally outrageous things in the heat of the moment.

Then Shelley had packed her things and left, taking their one and only car with her.

So here I am, Mike thought, now tying up the last of the legal contracts, my marriage on the rocks, wifeless and carless, yet most definitely, the innocent party.

How it had all transpired was a mystery.

Five minutes after Shelley had slammed the door behind her, he had phoned his parents to complain.

"Shelley's left me," he'd told his mother.

"She's what?"

"She walked out, left me in the lurch."

"Left you? Why? What have you done?"

"Well, I don't know. How should I know? It was her."

Parents have the gift of making you feel guilty even when you're as innocent as a new-born lamb.

"Think."

They give you one-word admonitions that can take you right back to kindergarten.

"I'm trying."

"Try harder."

They can insult and anger you, but you can't retaliate or they disown you with, "You're no son of mine" or words to that effect.

Eventually he'd managed to piece together the sorry situation, by which time he had the ears of both his mother and father.

"She'll be at her mother's. You must phone her, son. Say you're sorry," his father had said.

"No, I'm not doing that. I mean, she started it all."

So there.

"You're being silly, Mike," his mother said.

Typical. The son you said was the brightest lad in the whole school is now the village idiot.

"I won't phone her."

"Shall I?" his mother had asked.

"No! Promise me you won't do that, you won't phone her."

"All right, Mike. I promise I won't phone her, but . . ."

"I know — I'm being silly!" Mike had slammed down the phone.

Parents don't like it when a son takes command of his life and insists on making his own decisions and is no longer in need of their counselling.

MIKE picked up the finished contracts and walked through to the other office.

Benjamin Daniels regarded him with a jaundiced eye and muttered, "Huummph," which Mike took to mean that he had done a good job.

As he left Benjy's office, he was aware of a downward swing in his mood. It was his birthday, his parents' anniversary and a Red Letter Day, and he was feeling out-of-sorts, down-in-the-dumps, yeuch.

He hated to admit it, but he was missing Shelley.

He resisted the urge to phone her, reasoning that, as it was all her fault, she would come to her senses and phone him.

She didn't.

He spent the rest of the day trying to reinflate his ego, telling himself that he had been right in what he had said to Shelley. One of them had to be strong and clear-sighted enough to take a stand on what was best for both of them.

A baby, yes. Fine, in time. A second car, on the other hand, would be an asset now and it would be then, too.

He liked the way he put that. He glanced at his watch and wondered how long it would take him to walk home.

That evening, clutching a bouquet of flowers and the marvellous cut-crystal vase he and Shelley had chosen as an anniversary present, he took a taxi over to his parents' house.

How had his parents managed to stay married to each other for 30 years, he wondered. It was a curious and original thought for someone whose own marriage was teetering on the rocks of incompatibility.

That, he had decided, was as close as he could come to explaining Shelley's inexplicable behaviour.

He paid the taxi driver and rang his parents' doorbell. Maybe his parents, being born in a different time and all of that, knew something he didn't know about marriage? No, that was too vague, maybe . . .

The door was thrown open and he received a greeting worthy of the prodigal son before being pulled into the lounge.

The hi-fi was playing music from the 60s. His aunts and uncles and his parents' friends and neighbours were standing around in small, chatty groups with drinks in their hands.

And, sitting alone, on a small couch in the background, was Shelley.

Mike turned to stone. His heart began to thump like a piston and he felt the full and awful backlash of a double-cross.

"Mother, you lied to me! You promised you wouldn't invite Shelley," he hissed.

His mother smiled sweetly and said, "I didn't. Your father did."

MIKE decided he would just have to brazen it out. He went over and sat dumbly down beside Shelley on the couch. After a time they started talking, because there was nothing else they could do.

Shelley said she was sorry.

He said it was probably his fault.

She apologised again.

He told her that it was his fault and that he had missed her. After a moment he asked her why she had got so mad.

She smiled a slow, forgiving smile. "Because, Mike, I thought, as I was already six weeks pregnant, it might be a good idea for us to think about starting a family."

Mike felt himself go pale. He stared at Shelley with vacant eyes and a blank mind.

"Why didn't you tell me?" he said.

"Because, at the time, you were busy telling me I was as thick as two short planks . . ."

"Oh."

The news was beginning to sink in. Parenthood began to take on a whole new meaning.

"I'm going to be a father?" His thoughts were bouncing like ping-pong balls.

"Yes." Shelley nodded and laughed.

"Shelley, I love you."

"And I love you, Mike."

Mike looked up to see his mother and father standing at his side.

"Happy birthday, Mike," his mother said, while his father winked conspiratorially at Shelley.

Parents are something else. They never give up, do they? No matter what you think of them, they go on loving you and helping you and maybe even teaching you.

After all, that's their business. ∎

Leave It To Daddy!

by Anne Edgerley

Common sense . . . he reckoned that's all it would take to sort out our Christmas chaos. And I for one had more sense than to argue!

IT was Christmas Eve and I awoke with a blinding headache. Timmy, our youngest, was cutting his back teeth. I had been up half the night. Nick, my husband, had slept blissfully through it all, his senses dulled by the copious amounts of alcohol he had consumed at the office party the previous night.

"It's not fair," I muttered, pulling on my dressing-gown and listening uneasily to the sound of quarrelling voices floating up the stairs.

Christmas to Nick meant celebratory lunches for a fortnight, culminating in a booze-up at the office party, while I was lucky if I managed to snatch a cheese sandwich at lunchtime.

Whoever talked blandly about "the joys of the festive season" obviously wasn't a wife and mother with three over-excited children.

To make matters worse, over the last few days, the weather, true to form, had been horribly wet and windy, so that I couldn't even send them out into the garden to play. Instead, I had to devise endless games to keep them happy, at the same time making sure they didn't stumble on the presents stored away in various hiding places about the house.

As always I'd meant to start the preparations in good time but had got caught up in a welter of parties, carol concerts and Christmas shopping.

"Ice the cake, make mince pies, stuff the turkey, wrap up the presents," I muttered to myself. Thank heavens the shopping was finished!

I opened the kitchen door. The floor was covered with cornflakes.

"Just what has been going on here?" I demanded coolly.

"It was Michael's fault," Susy said aggrievedly. "He said he had to have the cornflakes first because he was the eldest and . . ."

"Well?" I asked forbiddingly.

"Well, I said I should have them first because I was a girl and . . ."

"And?"

"And the packet split."

I hauled Timmy out from under the table where he was happily consuming handfuls of dusty cornflakes in company with the dog and the cat, and dumped him in his high chair. Ignoring his vociferous protests, I scrunched across the room to get the dustpan and brush.

Nick came in then, whistling merrily. I glared at him. He'd been drinking and I had a headache. There was no justice in the world.

"Morning everyone. Good heavens, what's all that on the floor?"

"Cornflakes," I said briefly, filling the kettle.

Eventually everyone got something to eat. I fed Timmy his cereal resting my head on my hand. Nick actually noticed.

"You do look a bit under the weather, pet. If you'd only get yourself organised and not leave things until the last minute, you wouldn't get in such a state, would you?" he said, crunching toast loudly.

"And if you hadn't been in a drunken stupor, you'd have heard Timmy screaming his head off half the night!" I retorted.

He looked surprised. "Was he? I didn't hear a thing."

"Good for you," I said nastily.

He looked at me reproachfully. "Hey, where's your Christmas spirit?"

"It's buried beneath a mountain of chores," I complained bitterly.

"I've told you . . ."

"Nick," I said coldly, "if you tell me once more that I should organise myself, I swear — Christmas or no Christmas — I'll empty the milk jug over your head. Got it?"

The children looked hopeful, but disaster was averted by a thump in the hall as the last lot of Christmas cards thudded through the letter-box. Michael and Susy raced to fetch them, knocking over a stool en route and narrowly missing the dog, who had been lurking near the table hoping Timmy would drop something.

The dog yelped in panic, Timmy yelped in unison and my head buzzed.

Wearily, I got up from the table and went to look for the stuffing. I might as well start with the turkey, I thought unenthusiastically.

"Did you send the Johnsons a card?" Nick asked.

"No," I said, rummaging through the cupboard. Where on earth was the wretched stuffing?

"Well, they've sent us one. Have we got any left?"

"No . . . and even if we had, I spent half an hour yesterday queuing up in the Post Office for stamps, so the Johnsons will have to survive without a card from us."

"Don't you make a list?" Nick asked irritably.

"Of course I do." I still couldn't find the stuffing. Surely I hadn't put it in the fridge along with the turkey? I hadn't, but I had omitted to shut the fridge door properly and the dog obviously had designs on the turkey.

"No. No. No!" I yelled, just in the nick of time.

"What on earth!" Nick exclaimed.

"The dog's just about to lick the turkey. I've forgotten the bloomin' stuffing and you should have married someone more organised!" I screamed and burst into tears.

NICK got up and, crossing the room, put his arms around me and stroked my hair in the way he comforted Susy when she fell over. "What's the matter, darling?"

"I've got an awful headache," I sobbed. "I can't cope with Christmas as well."

"Come on," he said, taking me by the arm.

"Where to?" I sniffed.

"You're going back to bed. You're worn out."

I pulled away. "You must be mad. I haven't iced the cake, there's the mince pies to make and now I'll have to go out again and get the stuffing."

"Forget the mince pies," he said airily. "I'll make them!"

"You?" I said incredulously.

"No problem," he said loftily. "The recipe will be in all the cookery books, won't it? It just needs a little common sense. And don't worry — I'll get the stuffing," he added firmly, pulling back the bedclothes and sitting me down on the bed. I sank back against the pillows and shut my eyes for a moment. Nick came back with two soluble aspirins swirling around in a glass of water. "Drink that," he commanded briskly.

"Look, Nick, I can't possibly go to bed," I said weakly, taking the glass. "The children . . ."

He drew the curtains. "Lie down and don't be difficult," he said, tucking me in. I lay down anxiously. Of course he wouldn't be able to manage. He'd never be able to make the mince pies. I lay back and waited for the cry of help.

When I awoke, the clock was striking twelve and footsteps were coming up the stairs. Susy appeared in the doorway followed by Nick bearing a tray on which reposed a bowl of soup and a golden brown mince pie.

"How are you feeling?" he asked gently.

I considered. "Much better. Did you make this?"

"Of course!" he said breezily. "I told you there was nothing to it."

I gazed at him in stunned admiration and, if the truth were told, not a little chagrin.

I prided myself on my mince pies, but they did tend to come out of the oven looking a little lop-sided and the mincemeat sometimes oozed out. This pie was absolutely perfect.

"We've been making lists for Santa Claus. Do you want to see them?" Susy asked.

"Yes please," I said meekly.

Michael came in and they all sat on the bed. I snatched up the bowl of soup as it rocked perilously.

"Here's Timmy's list, Mum," Michael said.

"A drum!" I exclaimed in horror.

"He likes drums," Michael said defensively.

"Drums are out," Nick declared firmly.

"How do you know that Santa Claus hasn't got any drums, Daddy?" Susy asked with four-year-old innocence.

At the age of eight, Michael no longer believed in Santa Claus and was given to exaggerated nods and winks whenever his name was mentioned.

"Yes, how do you know, Dad?" he said, grinning.

I frowned at him. "What's on your list, Susy?"

"She wants a cowboy outfit," Michael said scornfully. "Whoever heard of a girl wanting a cowboy outfit?"

"What's wrong with it? Why can't I have one? If you can be a cowboy, why can't I?"

"Because you're a girl, stupid."

"That's enough," I said hurriedly. "I'm sure if Susy wants a cowboy outfit, Santa will try to find her one."

It had been wrapped up for months and hidden on top of our wardrobe. I understood how she felt. At her age I had wanted to be an engine driver.

Nick got up. "I'll take these two with me to do a bit of last-minute shopping," he announced.

"I won't take Tim if you don't mind. Making the mince pies exhausted him."

"We're going to look for a present for you," Susy confided in a stage whisper as they all trooped out of the room.

I got dressed and looked in on Timmy, who was sleeping peacefully, bits of pastry adhering to his fingers and hair. Downstairs everything was beautifully tidy and Nick had lit the fire.

However, his idea of tidying up amounted to stuffing everything into the nearest cupboard, as I found to my cost when a shower of toys descended on my head.

"So much for organisation," I muttered, going into the kitchen to ice the cake.

Nick and the children came back about four o'clock loaded up with glittering, exciting-looking parcels.

"You did get the stuffing?" I asked anxiously.

"Of course!" Nick grinned and collapsed in the chair. "I'm exhausted and I'm gasping for a cup of tea."

"You must be," I said, trying to sound sympathetic, although I couldn't help thinking how often on Saturday afternoons I struggled in with shopping and children to find him with his feet up in front of the TV and wondering what was for tea.